COVID
APOCALYPSE

PATRICK SIMS

WOUNDED HEALERS LLC.
EMPATHY-SOLIDARITY-UNDERSTANDING

Wounded-Healers.org

Published by Aleah Jean Publishing, Glen Burnie, Maryland
www.PublishedByAJ.com
ISBN 978-1-7379450-5-5
Copyright © 2022 by Patrick Sims

Printed in the United States of America

If I go crazy, then will you still call me superman?

- Three Doors Down

CONTENTS

PROLOGUE

The first bomb took them all by surprise; it exploded some meters away from where they stood, and they were swept up in the wind, forcefully tossed about like ragdolls by the sheer might of the blast.

Nicholas took the worst of the explosion. He was right in front of the group when it went off. Nicholas watched his life flash before his eyes as he was thrown against a car, hitting his head so hard it left him concussed as he fell to the floor with a loud thud. The serum bottle he clutched flew out of his hands-on impact, their last hope very nearly lost, but he quickly caught it before it could roll away from him, or worse, shatter. Bruised, bloodied, and tormented by the traumatic ringing in his ears, he dragged himself back onto his feet groggily. The heat had scorched him, though by some string of luck, the burns had not been too dire. Even if they were, he had no time to lick his wounds. It was a slow and grueling process, but there was no time to waste, too much was at stake, and the fate of many demanded that he survive. There might not have been that many left to save, tragically, but the people outside waiting on him were more than enough.

Nicholas hesitated; it was a miracle he had survived the first blast, a miracle that did not seem too likely to repeat itself if he were to hurry on blindly. He took a moment to regain his bearing and assess the mess he had found himself in… When it appeared that the bomb would not be repeated, he seized the opportunity to hurry over to his teammates. Throughout it all, Nicholas had refused to become acclimated to death as he checked on the others to make sure they were okay, reluctant to let another person die on him. He needed everyone safe.

It took him a moment, but eventually, Nicholas realized his right eye had been nipped, blurring his sight with blood, but he forced it open. The almost mind-numbing pain was accompanied by an unbearable throbbing at the back of his head, but he endured it, still searching eagerly through his teary left eye for a glimmer of hope. Flames had engulfed the path before them, and behind them came the agitated groans of the hoard approaching. Nicholas's search was not in vain. He thought he had noticed another passage they could take to the far left of the street down a tunnel.

He was frantic, as he hurried his team along with him, only to be halted at a pit of despair. They were running out of safe options to get away from their impending doom, and their only other alternative was the tunnel he had just noticed, and it was blocked. The blast that had disoriented Nicholas and his team had caused the entrance to cave in on itself, it would take forever to dig through the debris, and there was not enough time. Their original route had been blown to bits before their very eyes, and the only other passage left was destroyed.

They didn't have any other options, but they weren't ready to quit just yet. They had one last choice before them.

They must turn around.

CHAPTER ONE

THAT DIDN'T JUST HAPPEN

Staff Sergeant Nicholas Joseph David Sims was not in the best of moods. He woke up that morning feeling like his brain was going to split in half by the severe hangover tormenting him. He usually was not much of a drinker. Still, he had spiraled into an overwhelming sadness the night before, one that he was foolish to believe could only be pushed back by the burning euphoria of alcohol. However, as he sat in bed, he was engulfed by the sadness he had evaded and a bitter aftertaste on his lips. It was a brief feeling; reality had resumed once more, so he popped some painkillers and gurgled them down with Gatorade.

The alarm set for 5.30 am on his phone blared suddenly, causing him to wince in pain. He swept back his baby fro with one hand, using the other to turn off the alarm hurriedly. He missed, and it fell to the ground, ending its persecuting noise. Left to the silence, he took a deep breath of resolve; it was time to get ready for another workday.

Nicholas served the United States Air Force at Joint Base McGuire-Dix-Lakehurst, located in New Jersey where he worked as a Power Plant and Vehicle Technician for over five years. He had been recruited at a time when global tension had spiked, and the telltale signs of war reared their heads left, right, and center. He used to live at the base, and due to the increased airspace activity and the insurmountable pressure on the USAF and NATO, his work hours had become increasingly brutal and endless. Even though, he still counted himself lucky to get a high-end job as he did, despite how difficult the times had made finding them for everyone else. Hysteria was on the rise, and employers outright rejected hundreds of applicants daily, blaming it all on the fears that losing a war would cause them, a war that nobody was sure would come or not.

A lot had changed since then, and though such a time felt so long ago, the changes had not necessarily been for the better. With the outbreak of yet another variant of the SARS-CoV-2 in 2025, confirmed to be genetically combined and mutated with the Ebola virus, many countries quickly realized that better things could result from their foreign policy than a World War Three. There were meetings upon meetings where representatives of each country were given a fair hearing, trying their absolute best to develop solutions. The United Nations made increased efforts towards improving the status quo, but despite their hard work, several countries were still falling apart at the seams, leaving them with nothing more than patchwork to be done. Even the supposed superpower states were reminded of their stark mortality in the presence of an even greater pandemic. Every country was forced to stand on its own; there was no point assisting one another when they could hardly even control the situation within their borders. Faced with a horrifying death toll—the likes of which had never been seen, the world had been set on a path that bordered between anarchy and extinction.

Insecurity, civil unrest, and economic depression soon accompanied the pandemic, leaving the masses distraught. The ineffectiveness of lockdowns and other government programs only seemed to worsen the situation. The health systems of nations were overwhelmed, set on a steady decline in performance, no thanks to an explosive increase in anti-vaxxers and civil dissent, which steadily became rampant across the globe. 'World peace' became a utopian concept. Soon, extinction had begun to seem dreadfully plausible, with the global scale spike in suicide rates. But Nicholas, along with the rest of the world, knew that the worst was yet to come.

2027 arrived and met the few who still clung to dear life, as well as several others who, with great disappointment, had managed to survive. The world had changed in the worst way possible; no one could blame those who had fallen into depression during the pandemic for wanting to put an end to their misery, but with life was hope. So many banded together to pull through the worst of it.

The New Year had been welcomed poorly and, in what almost seemed like revenge, brought with it the umpteenth phase of the pandemic. The combined Coronavirus and Ebola virus, which the World Health Organization tagged the Hybrid-V-25, evolved into an even scarier disease when rabies was added to the melting pot. It truly felt like the gods above or below, whichever of them existed, were excessively enjoying their game of mix and match.

Three months had passed since the first outbreak in New York City. Covid Prime was spread by contact with the infected or any of their bodily fluids. By early March, it had wormed its way to the very ends of the earth. There was no country or state that could boast of having no victims of the disease. Even health centers that claimed to serve as sanctuaries had become hotbeds with infected staff.

The global pandemic had become an even greater crisis. At first, even the UN didn't know what to do, neither did the Heads of State nor any of the prominent medics who had once pushed out batch after batch of vaccines. Those vaccines had been taken by a lot of people, but unfortunately, there was no change. The virus had evolved, developing immunity to several vaccines. Things only seemed to go downhill when news broke out of a damning discovery that some of the vaccines administered to hundreds were expired. It created an uproar that could have very well been the spark that marked humanity's breaking point, with tensions raised to their utmost high. It was one thing to give out vaccines that had little to no effect against the virus, but another thing entirely to administer expired vaccines that only worsened the symptoms. Nobody knew what to do anymore because nothing worked; despair had found its way into the hearts of millions.

However, it was in humanity's darkest hour that a slim chance at salvation revealed itself. A nationally diverse team of scientists finally observed, in their secure facility, that the effects of the new virus could be the key to saving humanity. With their experiments done, things started to take a brighter turn with the hopes of a vaccine. They noted that the virus was not a sure killer. It either didn't survive against the immune system, or it successfully took root, gradually duplicating, not killing immediately, unlike its hybrid predecessor, which was somewhat of a relief.

With this newfound knowledge, the hope for a cure was somewhat restored. Governments determinately resumed pushing for vaccination research on the wide demographic of people who struggled with persisting symptoms. The people also co-operated as the Government seemed to be doing research on the one thing that had been plaguing humanity as a whole. The tension lessened for a while as there was restored energy in the air.

The U.S. government didn't hesitate to use or buy out any large venue they could find. The JB MDL had become a shadow of what it used to be, but the army hospital was still active. Even a section of Fort Dix was dedicated to housing and observing the infected. The remaining members of the armed forces and non-military medical staff were forced to protect themselves from head to toe as it was quite easy to get infected. Though they weren't going to be near them at all, it was still a relief. So, it took Nicholas longer than usual to get dressed.

An hour later, he stepped out the door all suited up, every surface of his skin safely secured beneath a layer of leather or plastic. Taking one last look at his apartment, which stared back at him silently, he wondered how he failed to notice how empty it'd become. Something felt off. Well, everything did. With a heavy sigh, he locked up and left.

The McGuire Air Force Base was practically a stone's throw away from where he lived in Wrightstown, and it took him just eight minutes to get there. Lucky for him as he was never late. After passing all the checkpoints, he parked his cement-colored Toyota Tacoma not too far from the flight line where the 305th Aircraft Maintenance Squadron was stationed. The biometric authentication machines checked him in before he reported to his Squadron Leader that he had resumed duty.

"Nicholas!" a voice called out to him merrily as he came out of the office, and he stopped, albeit with much reluctance. Not now, he thought.

"Sergeant Franco," he greeted the tall figure thundering towards him in a pure white protective suit not too different from the one he was in.

"Oh, come on, man, do I have to keep telling you to call me Josue?"

Tiago Franco, or Josue as he liked to introduce himself, was a Luso-American with a thick accent and even thicker skin. Not much fazed him as he mostly maintained the sly smile on his lips. Nicholas had wondered how he had been able to do that, as even when they had issues at work, his smile never wavered. It was somewhat creepy to him how someone could smile like a fool as much as Josue did. Nicholas couldn't help his inkling that Josue had something to hide behind his ever-gleeful exterior.

They were the same age, rank, and under the same squadron, but for some reason, Nicholas refused to understand why Josue had taken a liking to him. He was the one who had dragged all the aircraft mechanics out drinking in a global pandemic, so Nicholas didn't bother hiding his sour mood, partly caused by the head-splitting hangover he was still sobering from.

"You're probably the only one in the whole of McGuire who sticks so doggedly to the last name basis," Josue chuckled loudly, brown orbs twinkling, taking no offense to Nicholas's curt way of speaking. "How's the hangover?"

"Bad," he deadpanned as they left the building, hit by the warm rays of light. Climate change had accelerated over the years; very soon, that warmth would graduate to scorching heat. Luckily for them, half of their work was done away from the sun, so no one was unfortunate enough to get tanned or sunburned. The mass expanse of the maintenance hangar provided more than enough shade. He headed there, greeting other pilots along the way, doing his best not to pay too much attention to Josue's babbling.

"That's what you get for drinking too much, *meu amigo*. If you'd like, I could recommend one of my traditional hangover remedies. You know, there's this very—"

Nicholas stopped him, knowing he would go on and on otherwise, "Thank you, but there's no need."

"I mean it. It works like a charm." He clicked his tongue. "If you're not interested, I'm sure that rookie would be. What was his name again… Darwin? Da…Diego! He must be worse off after downing all those shots. I doubt he'd be able to show up for work today."

The mention of that name stung ever so slightly, but Nicholas ignored it. He was still struggling to come to terms with everything that had happened, the events of the previous day hitting him hard and unexpectedly, and was not ready to deal with this paroxysm of emotions. If only he could stop talking, he thought, moving slightly away from the man who couldn't read a room, following him still like an oversized puppy.

"*Mas espere um minuto*, the two of you are housemates. Why is your brother not with you? That rascal, did he actually skip?"

He didn't utter a single thing in response as they quietly walked into the 305th hangar. Josue finally took the hint, and though he refused to leave Nicholas to himself, he swiftly changed the topic, which he was glad for. Josue was not ready to let go of their conversation, and truly, there was no situation that could be too awkward for him to handle.

He started talking about how the U.S. had become Public Enemy #1 after the outbreak of the Cold Prime virus, seeing as the person responsible for its spread was an American citizen. According to him, a popular conspiracy theorist had called it that in one of their videos, and the name stuck. It didn't help that during the first-ever COVID-19 outbreak, the then President had made sure to point fingers at everyone else. Nicholas could remember how it had been a bad move that had created a train of scathing words all over the globe. They butted heads, ones who supported the Government and those who condemned his words and actions. Nicholas tried not to think of it most of the time; after all, it was far too late to change the past.

"With the way things are going, all hell will break loose eventually. At this point, the world is too fucked up to salvage anything. What if we have to go to war?"

Unfortunately for Josue, Nicholas had already tuned him out by that time and was focused on running diagnostics on the RC-26 metro that had been brought in over the weekend. He really didn't care much about politics and also didn't care about the thought of war. The Government was elected to look into it, and whatever would happen, would happen. All that mattered at that moment was his work, which he focused on devotedly.

The other mechanics snickered at the scene. They all knew that once workaholic Staff Sergeant Nicholas Sims entered his zone, there was no dragging him out of it. Even when an interesting topic was being discussed, Nicholas was not outspoken. He never saw the need to raise his own opinion, preferring to keep to himself.

Josue 'hmphed' in defeat and decided to get some of his work done too.

A few hours passed, with everyone working tirelessly. As the workload was much, it was better for all hands to be on deck so as to gain more progress. Truthfully, the military had begun preparations to preempt any infiltration or incursion as the U.S. was facing serious public backlash. It was not easy being at the butt of other countries' jokes and insults. The country had already suffered these past seven years greatly, they couldn't risk taking any more damage.

At half-past one, the 305th Squadron Leader, Chief Steven Pesute, dropped by to check on them and announced their lunch break. Nicholas busied himself as his colleagues scattered in different directions, some heading to the Halvorsen Dining Hall, others to the few fast-food restaurants that were still open in their run-down mini-metropolis. He alone remained, tinkering distractedly with another aircraft.

Anyone who saw him would think him odd. He was meant to be

having a meal or taking a rest, but food was the last thing on his mind. Instead, he was wondering whether or not he should go and see Diego at the 905th's maintenance hangar. Their conversation the night before had not ended well, so he didn't know how things would go if he did. He continued his work, lost in thought as he debated with himself about what to do when he eventually got out of work.

Minutes passed by with him trapped in this back and forth within his mind. Suddenly, the whole place erupted into a troubling tumult of screeching and snarling.

What in the world?

Nicholas immediately stood on alert. From the clamor, he could make out the heavy sounds of frenzied footsteps, things crashing down or being torn apart, and an indescribable groaning. It sounded human, yet it was too animalistic and wild for him to say what it was for certain. Like a cat before a storm, Nicholas was on edge. Sensing that something had gone wrong, he subconsciously reached out for his Glock, safely tucked away beneath his belt, the safety still on. He doubted he would need it, but he took it along with him anyway. Nicholas always kept his service pistol hidden in his belt holster, although both were currently buried inside his protective suit. He decided against removing it as he warily approached the entrance. He had to blink a couple of times to adjust to the harsh brightness of the outside, his hazel brown eyes slowly taking in the appalling sight before him.

The military was being attacked not by enemy troops but by hordes of —U.S. civilians! No wonder he was yet to hear the sound of gunshots. Something caught his attention, making him pause. At first glance, they looked like people, but other than their build and the fact that they were plainly dressed (for those that still had their clothing intact), these haggard creatures hardly resembled normal human beings. They were of a sickly gray complexion, their skin dried to the dermis and peeling, almost sliding off every time they moved. They were accompanied by a god-awful stench, almost as though they had all just strolled out of a morgue.

It was a terrible sight that made Nicholas step back a bit in disbelief, recoiling at the stench in the air. Their movements were slow and strange. They swung their limbs about wildly and awkwardly, throwing each foot in front of the other with little to no coordination, almost as though they were just learning to walk. Rather, they had no control over their muscles but still had enough strength to grab forcibly at their human counterparts like they had vice grips for arms. It was as though they were puppets with no strings attached to them, eagerly pursuing everyone they came across with a cold dead look in their eyes. When they did manage to catch someone, they…aggressively proceeded to devour them.

Nicholas was momentarily stupefied at the trauma as he watched several of these creatures latch onto Airmen, gruesomely digging their loose-hanging jaws into them, most aiming for their necks. He could tell that they bit down hard, growling excitedly as they then ripped off chunks of flesh with each hungry bite. He took another step back instantly, snapped back to reality by the bone-chilling realization that he could be next.

That didn't just happen.

He was still in doubt, though he had paled from fear as it continued to unfold before his very eyes.

He thought for a second that his hangover was so bad he was day-dreaming and closed his eyes, taking deep calm breaths as he did. He prayed ever so desperately for the horrors to be nothing more than a bad dream, but sharp cries pierced the air around him, snapping him back to the reality he refused to confront. He opened his eyes in a jolt to see the…he didn't even know what to call them as they feasted ravenously on the unfortunate airmen. He instinctively reached out to help, but no one was near him, and everyone he could recognize had been ensnared in the crushing hold of these carnivorous creatures. It was a chaos that he could not comprehend.

"Nicholas!" He snapped his head to the right. Josue came running from that way, and for the first time in all their years of working together, Nicholas was thoroughly glad to see him, roughed up but in one piece.

Unfortunately, his yelling had attracted the monsters' attention, and some grunted at them, eyes staring blankly in their direction. Nicholas then noticed how they stood with their head cocked to the side as if they were trying to listen for the voice. He turned to Josue, shaking his head furiously when he saw his mouth move, but that didn't stop Josue from yelling a second time.

"Block the entrance to the hangar! *Ja!*" he spat out, ignoring Nicholas's strange action.

Nicholas ran back inside immediately, flipping the switch used to bring down the gates to the hangar without a moment's hesitation. Josue slid underneath just before the gates clamped down on the arm of a monster that had seized him. Its congealed blood splashed everywhere as its hand flew off. Half of the arm was near the gate, while the other half was sure to be fixed onto the owner.

"Oh shit, I hope it didn't scratch me," he mumbled after catching his breath, wiping the purplish-red goo he had been doused in off his mangled suit.

Nicholas, who had stood too far to share in his fate, gave him a minute to clean up while he calmed himself down. "What on earth is going on?"

"You think I fucking know?" Josue stretched out his arm, wanting to be pulled up. Nicholas helped him to his feet. "I'm on my way to Burger King when those…things show up out of nowhere, howling and growling in everybody's faces. It was utter chaos! We couldn't even fight back 'cause they're civilians—"

"How do you know that?" Nicholas started. "Did they look like normal civilians to you? Why were you concerned about them scratching you?"

"Didn't you notice? They're the people staying at the quarantine center," Josue replied to Nicholas's grim realization. "Each and every one of them. They all have tags, and a sizable number of them were even wearing hospital gowns. I don't know what's happened to them or how they broke out, but they're going crazy! They were scratching and biting, and anyone I saw who was lucky enough to survive their clutches started acting weird and going crazy too. Epa, Porra! When the fuck did cannibalism become a symptom of the Covid Prime virus?"

Nicholas was more than surprised to find out that those creatures were actually patients from Fort Dix, but that little bit of information only seemed to make matters worse. He took a deep breath and tried to put two and two together. The world knew little to nothing about the virus, so it was possible that it could completely rewire the human body. Some part of it had probably festered all this time, and with all the experimental vaccines they had been testing, it had started causing its victims to go on a deranged rampage. Assuming Josue was not wrong about all of them being infected, that would explain why those who had gotten attacked were also acting up. It had always been highly contagious.

The more he thought about it, the harder it was to believe. He couldn't exactly say for sure that something like this had never occurred in the entirety of human history. He had read about the drug that drove junkies to cannibalism in Miami decades ago, but in all his 24 years of life, he had never heard about anything that could turn fully-fledged human beings into flesh-loving, half-dead monsters.

"It's almost as if they're zombies," Josue chuckled bitterly, then gasped as if having a eureka moment. "What if they actually are?"

Nicholas ignored him. Other than the commotion outside, which he couldn't really hear over the air raid sirens, loud thuds could be heard from the gates. The sounds were akin to people banging their heads against a wall but in unison. He felt like the world was finally ending, and he had forgotten something important. It was a weird gut feeling that grew stronger by the second, and he couldn't figure out why.

"Come on, buddy, listen to me. I swear I'm on to something."

He thought hard about it before he finally realized.

"Sergeant Franco!"

"Sergeant Sims!" Josue replied automatically, startled by his shouting.

"Did you see Airman Arretta?"

"Who?"

"Airman Diego Arretta, from the 905th!"

Nicholas felt exasperated by the obvious confusion on his face. "The one you were talking about earlier…for God's sake, my brother!"

"Ai, the lightweight. I didn't see him." Josue shrugged. "You know, I was running for my life out there. Not much time to stare at people's faces."

Nicholas had expected that and sighed inwardly. He could feel the virulent pumping of his heart against the fear and anxiety that weighed down on it heavily. He didn't want to think about it. In fact, he didn't need to think about it. He unzipped his suit and promptly took out his gun. With no time to waste, he took off the safety and cocked it as he made a little resolution.

"I'm going back outside."

CHAPTER TWO

JOINT BASE
MCGUIRE-DIX-LAKEHURST

Josue didn't look shocked in the least bit. Instead, he smirked at him knowingly, acting as if Nicholas had not just announced his death wish. "Whatever, but even if you don't believe me, I've watched a couple of Zombie movies, so I know a few things." It almost sounded as if he were bragging. "Don't use the gun unless you have to. You saw their reaction; loud noises and bang-bangs like that get their attention. We need better weapons."

We?

Nicholas was honestly taken aback by Josue's declaration. "You think you can open those gates and just leave me here to become rot?" Josue scoffed. "Grab whatever you can find from the aviation kits, and let's go."

Nicholas was skeptical about Josue coming along with him, but Nicholas was the one about to put him in danger, and he'd made a point about how he couldn't leave Josue behind, so he didn't exactly have the right to complain.

Walking over to where they kept the toolboxes, he kicked one open. After a moment of thought, he brought out a pneumatic air rivet gun and shoved it into his multi-holster. He also took a large torque wrench to carry in his other hand. He concluded that any more would be a burden and might slow him down in a fight.

On the other hand, Josue seemed to operate by an entirely different logic as he stuffed a backpack full of water bottles from the fridge and a bunch of tools he had deemed worthy as weapons, amongst other things.

"What?" he said defensively, his hands trembling almost unnoticeably as they gripped a crowbar. "If we don't die within the first few minutes, then we need all we've got, so please don't give me that look."

Nicholas nodded, zipping his suit fully. "We're heading straight for the 905th's hangar. Don't wait till the gates are fully up. Once they're high enough, run out when I give the signal and keep running. It might count as self-defense but avoid attacking them. You might get caught up in actually doing some damage, but you could end up surrounded in the process."

Josue mock-saluted in response, and they both headed over to where the switch. The pounding on the gates had increased, meaning the hoard outside was getting larger, and they could hear the frustrated growls of the creatures lurking behind, making them hesitate.

"Should we pray?" Josue mumbled feebly.

Nicholas flipped the switch, his unuttered refusal.

The gates began to rise with a start, and the growls intensified in confused delight. A rotten stench overpowered their noses; they staggered backward. Nicholas held his breath and quickly counted the number of feet that had appeared. It was hard to tell from their frantic movements, but he estimated at least nine of them were standing just beyond the gates. He noticed a big enough gap between the fifth and sixth pair of feet that they could use without letting the doors recline fully. They would have to be extremely fast. Once he had the full view of their distorted lower bodies, he gestured to Josue and whispered, "Now!"

They darted towards the gates. Crouching slightly, they slipped through the open space, ignoring the creatures. The half-humans felt something glide past them but could not react in time. By the time they could turn their stiff necks to see that it was their prey, Nicholas and Josue had disappeared into the chaos.

As he ran, Josue almost couldn't believe his eyes at the sight of all the corpses splattered all over the ground—or rather, their remains. The ones who hadn't yet been dismembered were being ripped apart ruthlessly by these animals, right in front of his eyes, with many of them donning military uniforms. It was a horrendous scene that made their hearts sink for a moment.

Nicholas had feared the worst, but even then, the scene dazed him, but only for temporality. "Come on!" Nicholas called to Josue harshly, snapping him out of a trance he hadn't realized he had fallen into. As they ran, making their way as quickly as possible to the 905th hangar, they passed a pile of bodies when someone latched onto Josue's leg, pulling him to the ground. Nicholas was as equally shocked as Josue, nearly darting over to help him back on his feet when they both realized it was not one of the creatures that had latched onto him. A man was struggling to get out from underneath the pile. He used his other hand to support himself and was trying to drag himself out right before they came running past him.

"Son!" he desperately called out for Josue. "Help me!" His voice had summoned a near horde of the creatures, and Josue felt obligated to help the man. Nicholas had no intention of getting on the floor to join them, but he waited with his wrench propped up as a melee to buy them time if he needed to.

Josue swiftly took a firm grip of the man's arm and pulled him with all his might as the man pushed himself with all the strength he could muster. In a moment, he was free from beneath the corpses, but then Josue stared down in shock as it dawned on him—the man had already lost his legs. Where his legs used to be, there were chewed-up stumps; it was obvious that the creatures had gotten to him long before they did. He screamed in horror as he struggled to free himself from the desperate man's grasp. The man was still very much alive, pleading, yelling, and begging at the top of his lungs as Nicholas helped Josue back onto his feet. They left him to a mob that descended on him mere moments after they got away.

The creatures were everywhere, either strolling about aimlessly on their own or shuffling together in large hordes. They were hardly any of them on their path, though. They had probably dispersed to capture more prey or were already feeding in clusters. It wasn't hard to weave through the few hordes that had noticed them. At least that was what they thought until two lunged at Josue from the corner of their eyes. Fear seized him as they tackled him to the ground, snarling and clawing at his suit. He barely managed to keep their teeth out of his face with the crowbar he clutched firmly as he swung at them. Josue cried out desperately as Nicholas returned to his rescue, taking one of them by surprise, smashing his wrench into the side of its head, spilling the contents of its skull across the pavement. Then Nicholas ripped his wrench through the aperture of the other one before tugging Josue free.

"Did they bite you?" Nicholas snapped, his free arm grasped tightly about Josue's collar.

Josue was still dazed, sputtering as he patted himself down, "N-No! Thank God! No!"

"Keep going!"

A third popped up in front of Nicholas while they were distracted. He dodged as its hand snatched at the hem of his sleeve. He dug his left elbow into its wrist and used the butt of his gun to smack its shoulder blade, propelling it away from him. His ears picked up the sound of slurred words. He turned to see a woman speaking to him from the floor.

"Help…me." She tried to reach out to him but was unable to do so. If all of her limbs were missing, how did she crawl 'a good distance'? Before laying where she did, surrounded by a pool of her own blood. Her skin had paled from blood loss, and half her hair had already fallen off; he could see that she had already started decaying. She was infected just like all the others. It was too late. She would either turn soon or die in the process, but he couldn't tell her that. From the look in her eyes, she already knew. It was too late to save her, but he could still help her.

Josue hid his face as Nicholas mouthed the word "sorry" before firing his Glock in her face, putting an end to her misery.

The hangar was some way down the flight line, and his gunshot had announced their arrival, so Nicholas and Josue kept on running as hard as they could, pushing back the creatures that threw themselves their way, doing their absolute best to ensure neither of them was ambushed again. Nicholas could see a couple of them shuffling in and out of the entrance, and his stomach sank. Still, he refused to imagine the worst.

"The crowbar, let's switch!"

He twisted slightly, switching his gun to his left hand so he could toss it towards Josue, then caught the tool flung at him the next second with a seasoned warrior's proficiency. This time, there was no space they could squeeze through. He readied himself to face them head-on, but Josue unexpectedly sprinted past him.

"I'll create an opening for you, but, *meu amigo*, you have to hurry!" he yelled, diving forward, throwing a bunch of the tools in his backpack at the small hoard that had trudged towards him from the entrance. They groaned when hit as if they were cursing him. Broad-shouldered and stoutly built, with plenty of close-combat experience, he gave a sense of assurance. Swinging the claw hammer in his other hand at them, he made a small opening, and Nicholas zipped through.

Nicholas spared a glance back at Josue, who managed to call out to him, "I can take them on, so—look behind you!"

Nicholas barely managed to move back in time as a cold hand grabbed at him, ripping through his protective suit. It tore off a huge piece of the shirt he was wearing underneath with it, leaving an area of his torso exposed. He was scared white, but entertained a moment of relief when he realized its attack had not broken skin or so much as bruised him. It came at him a second time, lunging forward with desperation fueled by hunger. He struck it with the crowbar, hooking a chunk of its loose skin, yanking it clean off. Thick blood with the same purplish hue as all the others spilled from its wound, but it continued its relentless attack as though it had been unscathed. This one in particular, seemed more alive than dead with the way its yellow eyes glowered. It bellowed at Nicholas, and he stepped back before charging at it again.

There were two more behind the one that had attacked him. To his luck, they were both engrossed in feasting inside the hangar. He decided the sooner he was done with the one before him, the better. He swung the crowbar at its neck, putting a lot of strength in his recoil. With a sharp crack, its head came off, whorling towards one of the planes. Nicholas forced himself to repress the waves of guilt that washed over him. Its body was still moving, so he shoved it aside and pressed forward.

Wiping off his sweat, he cast a worried look around the hangar. *Where on earth could Diego be?* There were very few half-human creatures here and hardly any dead bodies. A good sign, he hoped. Then doubt that there was ever anyone in the hangar crept in as another creature lunged at him while he was lost in thought. Nicholas was swift, holding the crowbar between its teeth before it could descend on him. After battering it to the ground, he decided to check the planes before others noticed him, unable to recognize any of the corpses.

Nicholas heard footsteps and looked back to see Josue jogging to meet him, backpack bouncing behind him. His clothes were shredded, and his black curls, along with the rest of him, were smeared with goo, but he appeared unharmed, making quick work of the others that Nicholas had initially avoided.

"We don't have much time," Josue panted heavily as he joined Nicholas, the sound of dragging feet not far behind. "I'll fend off the ones outside while you go see if he's in any of the cargo planes."

A keen sense of solidarity replaced some of the guilt Nicholas had been feeling when he noticed Josue still trembled as he clutched the wrench in his hands, though his stern gaze held a confident resolve. He nodded in response, then ran towards the C-130J Super Hercules, which had one of its doors ajar, as Josue widened his stance, prepared to attack.

The last half-human insight stood at the bottom of the steps, struggling to make its way up. Its body was far more decayed than the others; bones had started to jut out of its greenish-gray flesh, sparsely covered by the hospital gown it had on. Compared to all the others, it looked like it had been dead long before its reanimation. It turned its colorless eyes in Nicholas's direction and grunted at him, exuding a foul odor. It was a deep vicious sound. Without a moment's hesitation, Nicholas hacked at its shoulder with his crowbar, but a missing arm didn't hinder it much. With its other fairly good arm, it lunged forward and managed to snatch the crowbar out of his hands. He was forced back by its strength; all the creatures they had encountered displayed an almost inhumane amount of it, but the one before him was in a league of its own, which came as a shock to Nicholas.

This one was indeed unlike the others he had fought. It released the crowbar as if knowing it had not caught onto flesh and attacked again. Nicholas knew that all it needed to do was latch onto him to make him a goner, so he quickly ducked, snatching up the crowbar as he did, and used it to hook its calf so he could haul its lower left leg off. Purple goo splattered on him as it half-kneeled on the ground. It continued to sway and grunt at him despite the fact that it was more or less immobile. Nicholas had already decided to leave it be and continue up the steps, but it swung at him again, and this time it caught hold of his suit. Its nails swiped at his exposed skin as it dragged him back; his eyes widened in alarm. He bit down on his tongue to stop himself from shouting out in pain as it dug its nails deeper into his stomach. He kicked at it and, with much effort, finally broke free from its iron-clad grip.

"Shit," Nicholas cursed as he felt the open wound around his abs, knowing he was done for. Picking up the crowbar, he thrust it into the creature's head with a loud thwack. In a pained fury, he retrieved the crowbar from its skull and proceeded to beat it repeatedly till its head became a mash of bone and brain matter, and the soft rotten tissue had formed a thick slimy coat on the head of the crowbar. He didn't stop until its incessant roars died out, and it finally stopped thrashing about. He had completely desiccated its head.

Soaked in sweat and goo, Nicholas panted as he bent over his victim. The state of his weapon and the sight before him disgusted him to the point of throwing up as he squeezed his eyes shut. The smell of rotten organs surrounded him; he felt like he was being suffocated by it and the stifling guilt that he could no longer force back down. He struggled for a few more minutes, trying desperately to calm himself. After taking one, or two, or seven deep breaths, Nicholas straightened himself and opened his eyes again.

He glanced down at his abdomen, examining the wound. The skin around it had peeled off, but it was not bleeding that much. It was not a deep cut, but it was an injury, nonetheless. Despite the pain, he didn't feel any different, although it was too soon to conclude anything. Having already wasted a lot of time, Nicholas decided to remove it from his mind and move on. He had toed the line between life and death too many times to be bothered. He tore off a bit of his sleeve and used it to bandage the wound.

Nicholas shook off the grime on his tools before he ascended the steps. His eyes swept over the interior as he entered the plane, making sure that there was no other creature out to get him. The Hercules was not too long, and he briskly walked down to the tail of the plane. He checked everywhere but found nothing and no one. There was no random leg or arm lying about, or any of the telltale signs of tragedy that the creatures trailed everywhere they went.

He became increasingly perplexed. *Had nobody thought to hide here?* Nicholas pondered in disbelief as he went back to the entrance he had come in through. The last half-human had been found quite far from the others. It had been so determined to climb into the plane. *Why would it struggle to enter if it was not going after somebody?* It might have just been an attempt to pacify himself, but he felt like things weren't adding up.

Nicholas paused, noticing something in his peripheral view. There were bloodstains on the floor leading all the way to the cockpit. He almost thought they were his until he realized they were brown and had dried already. He rushed forward with a sudden burst of hope and pushed open the door to the cockpit. Leaning against the control board was a lanky-looking man in yet another white protective suit. Well, it couldn't exactly be called white anymore with the amount of blood that had seeped through the bottom leg. The brown curls on his lowered head were matted, partially covering his face, but Nicholas recognized him immediately. His knees went weak with relief, and he fell to the floor as he cried out, "Diego!"

The other jolted awake at the sound of his name, head lulling as he came to. His hazel orbs flickered with different emotions as he looked around, trying to grasp the situation he was in. At the sight of Nicholas, the shock in them vivid, he gazed at him skeptically.

"Why…Why are you here?"

Nicholas needed a moment to collect himself, so didn't answer right away. He had been tense for so long that it felt weird to finally have his worries lifted.

"I had to make sure you were alive. Do you remember why *you* are here?"

"Somewhat," Diego breathed out, wincing as he adjusted himself and sat upright; he'd lost a lot of blood and was feeling partly anemic. "I was hiding from…some monsters? What?"

Nicholas could see how bewildered he was at his own memories and almost laughed. "Take it slow. There's no need to doubt yourself."

He nodded slowly, staring hard at Nicholas. "You…"

"No need to explain what's going on, I know. I'll fill you in on everything when you're a bit more conscious. For now, do you remember anything about your leg injury?"

"I was going to say you smell bad, but that too. And I think I fell, maybe something…cut me."

Nicholas knew he smelled awful, so he said nothing. He was more concerned about Diego's ankle, which he feared had been scratched, but there was not enough time to properly check the injury.

Josue was still out there. "Do you think you can walk?"

Diego tried to get up but fell back again. His ankle was swollen, and he was too weak to bear the pain. He shook his head in dismay.

Nicholas pinched the bridge of his nose and tried to work out a plan. Although he had wanted to go and observe the situation outside the air force base, there was no way he would leave Diego behind. Carrying him was out; he had to be able to fight freely, plus he was also tired. Staying in the plane seemed like the safest option available for them.

"I'll have to leave you here, Rio, but only shortly. After, I need you to lock the door, but don't stress yourself if you can't do it."

Diego glared at him with what little strength he had. "Don't call me…I don't need you talking down to me. I…I can manage even that."

Nicholas had not forgotten about their fight, and it seemed Diego had not either. He choked out his next words, feeling slightly dispirited, "I'll knock four times, so you know it's me. If I'm not back in—"

"Just go." Diego rolled his eyes. "Don't make me…wait for long."

Nicholas blinked, smiling for the first time that day. It was a soft smile that didn't fade even after he left.

CHAPTER THREE

COVID PRIME

Nicholas joined Josue outside, and together they battled against the last of the horde that had gathered at the 905th. There had only been a handful of them remaining, so even though they were exhausted, and he injured, they succeeded in killing off all of them, but they had no time to celebrate. Their little victory would pale if the full onslaught of infected were to find their way to the 905th. Nicholas had to rid himself of the guilt that held him back earlier as there was no other way to deal with them effectively than to butcher their brains and bodies. Nonetheless, the realization that he was basically murdering his colleagues and the citizens he served—and in such a gruesome way too—messed with his mind. Josue tried to be his usual cheerful self, but he had yet to forget the legless man he had left to the horde. They were both glad the fight ended as quickly as it did.

The moment Nicholas served the finishing blow to the very last one, Josue collapsed on the ground; the strength that had been holding him up had finally left him. He'd not had a moment of rest all afternoon and was too tired to be happy about his survival. Nicholas plopped down next to him, also in need of a break. His stomach hurt from the excessive movement, but he took the fact that he had not become a bloody, rotting mess like all the others as a good thing.

They sat there for a while before Josue broke the silence. "You called me 'Josue' out there. Did you know that was the first time in all our years of working together?" he laughed dryly. "Does that officially make us wingmen now?"

Although Nicholas didn't think they had experienced much together, this incident being their first time working as partners, he gave in and nodded. "Thanks…Josue," he mumbled meekly, then rose to his feet. "Don't call me your Wingman." The other laughed on, feeling exhilarated. "It's already evening. I'll go check if the coast is clear."

"*Meu amigo*, I think it's best if we spend the night in the cargo plane," Josue replied, getting up too. "Let's give it some time. Zombies tend to stick together. If you step out now and see even one, that's a sign that the whole damn horde isn't far behind."

How many zombie movies has this guy watched?

"I was thinking the same, but because Diego's hurt."

"Then it's better we don't risk going outside right now. If you make one wrong move and catch their attention, we're done for. Also, we don't know how strong their sense of smell is. I watched one movie…"

Seriously, how many?

"Let's go then."

Nicholas returned, exasperated with Josue, to the plane. They had taken a while trying to barricade the door as best as they could. He made sure all the entrances to The Hercules were closed off as well before they headed to the cockpit. When he tapped on the door four times, it took a little while before Diego opened up. He rested against the wall, face damp with sweat as he leaned on his uninjured left foot. Nicholas immediately moved him gently to the pilot's seat.

"I told you not to stress yourself."

"Shut up."

Josue chuckled by the door. "*Ai*, how could I forget? The hot-headed rainbow."

Diego looked surprised to see him. "Sergeant Franco," he greeted weakly, observing their difference in rank.

Diego had just been recruited and was still on the E-1 rank, but Josue lazily waved it off. "Please. Call me Josue."

"Yes...sir."

"It must run in the blood." Josue clicked his tongue. "Well, I'm going to take a piss and then nap. If you need anything, I'm your man."

"Sergeant...Josue," Nicholas called out to him before he disappeared down the corridor. "Do you have any first aid in that bag of yours?"

"Of course I do. Come along."

Returning to the cockpit with a bottle of water and a bunch of first aid materials, he tended to Diego's wound. It was a clean-cut and deep, as if something had neatly sliced into him. Thankfully, it had stopped bleeding. Comparing it to his wound, Nicholas doubted Diego had gotten it from a zombie (he had finally decided to accept Josue's way of referring to them). Nicholas felt relieved. He used this time to explain everything that had happened so far, stopping at intervals to let Diego assimilate to it all.

"Let's move you to the fuselage. You can rest better there."

Diego eyed him incredulously. "You...won't you attend to your wounds?"

"What? Nicholas is wounded?" Josue called out from behind. "Since when?"

"It's nothing, just a scratch," he said matter of factly as he slung Diego's left arm over his shoulder, dragging him forward.

Diego was about an inch taller at 6'3, but when limping, he appeared shorter, which, for some reason, he didn't like. He was glad when Nicholas let go of him to settle him in one of the sidewall seats.

Josue had taken off what was left of his suit and donned his plain clothes, which were also ripped here and there. He walked over to where they were, looking displeased. "I can't believe I'm just noticing it now. Let me see the wound."

Nicholas reluctantly pulled down the top half of his suit and raised his shirt, revealing, among his numerous scars, the bandage he had wrapped around himself. He untied it and let it fall, warranting a gasp from Josue.

"This isn't just a scratch!"

There were three prominent indents in Nicholas's stomach, which had been bruised a purple-red, contrasting with his pale skin. A bit of that skin had been torn off, exposing the pink lining of his flesh. It looked horrible and extremely painful.

Diego couldn't stand the sight of it, shifting his gaze back to Josue, who had started yelling, "Fuck! Is this what one of those zombies did to you? Why didn't you tell me?"

"It wasn't important."

"Nicholas!"

Lowering his shirt, he shook off his suit. "Sergeant Josue Franco. I'm fine. It will heal. I've been through much worse." That last comment made Diego flinch, unwanted memories of their childhood popping up in his mind.

"It isn't fine." Josue shook his head grimly. "A zombie did that to you. There's no way you haven't been infected. I told you what I saw out there. You saw it too, with your own two eyes! If that happens to you—"

"We don't know for sure." Nicholas held his head, feeling a nasty headache coming on. "I still feel more or less the same. Worst case scenario, you'd have to kill me. If that time comes, don't hesitate, just take me out before I hurt any of you."

The other two gaped at him disbelievingly. Diego, in particular, was furious. "You speak of death so easily. Does your life mean that little to you?" He started coughing. Nicholas returned to his side at once.

"Calm down. Don't overexert yourself."

Diego tried shoving him backward, but it ended up being a weak push. Nicholas sighed. "We might not be killers, but we signed up for this work knowing that anything could happen and we'd be dead on the spot. It's nothing to get worked up about. Josue, I'm counting on you to do the needful if things go wrong. For now, let's not argue about it. Everybody get some rest."

Josue remained silent, a torn look on his face. After a couple of seconds, he moved towards the cockpit and came back with the first aid. "Let me help you treat your wound, at least."

Nicholas was grateful but turned him down, not wanting to bother him any further. Josue insisted, pulling him to the floor where he also sat down, then got to work after sanitizing his hands. Positioning Nicholas on his back, he wet the dressings before applying them to the wound. He made sure to do it as delicately as he could, but Nicholas still grimaced with pain. Josue rolled some plastic wrap over the dressing and around his abdomen, then helped him stand up when he was through. Nicholas was patched up as best as he could get for the meantime.

"Thanks."

Josue said nothing, just tossed him another bottle of water from his bag, this time for drinking. Nicholas sat down next to Diego, who had already started dozing off, nodding stubbornly, refusing to give in to his fatigue. It made him laugh a bit. They weren't even blood brothers and had nothing between them that could make them a real family anymore, but Diego was all he had. He was not going to take for granted the fact that they were all alive. He never had.

Nicholas became preoccupied, thinking about how he had killed for the first time, when he too fell into a deep, uncomfortable sleep, afraid to see the deformed faces of the people he had to kill to get there. Normally, he didn't dream, but that day his mind traveled far away, taking him back to the days before he had been separated from his parents, and he was just the average kid. He looked around seven or eight years old and was busy playing in the front yard of his home. His mom watched over him from her seated position on the porch. Even in the dreamscape, Nicholas could not envision her properly. Her face had become a blur buried amongst distant memories, and although he knew she was speaking to him, the sound of her voice floated in waves that died out before reaching him. His dad was nowhere to be seen, as usual, and the dream started and ended with that still scene.

Nicholas woke up to the ferocious grumbling of his stomach. As he rubbed his eyes, he realized he had not eaten since that morning. They lacked food supplies, so he drank a lot of water instead. It was a temporary solution, but he'd have to settle for it, seeing as they couldn't leave the Hercules yet. He wondered what time it was, then remembered that his phone was actually in his pants pocket, along with his car key. Nicholas had completely forgotten that he had it on him.

He brought his phone out, surprised that it was still in one piece after the rough day he'd had. He was even more surprised to see that it was still connected to the McGuire AFB Wi-Fi. The time read 9:19 pm, so he figured he had been passed out for a long time. He checked his social media to see if there had been any updates regarding the situation. The military group chats had nothing. In contrast, all over his Twitter were posts talking about how the world was finally ending. Many of them were tagged with #ZombieApocalypse and #Covid Prime. He found out that similar incidents had occurred not just in America but all across the globe. He saw some clips that captured the whole thing live. After watching one where the person videoing ended up getting eaten, he stopped opening them. They only left him with a dreadful sense of anxiety.

From what he had read, the first set of people to turn into zombies had all been carriers of the Mutated virus. Most of them, especially their earliest victims, had been experiencing worsened symptoms, such as heightened aggression, delirium, skin decay, and loss of speech and mobility. It had been going on for a few weeks before they finally lost it. He saw a popular post speculate that the virus caused severe encephalitis and damaged the amygdala and hypothalamus.

The U.S. government had acknowledged the incident on their page and apparently in a press release too, though it was obvious that the situation was yet to be contained. Millions of people had been infected in the States alone, and those millions were rampaging, turning others into zombies. Although no concrete information had been provided, Nicholas felt it was safe to assume that Franco's theory was correct.

It was a lot to process. Putting his phone aside, he turned to see if the others were up yet. Josue was out cold on the floor, snoring loudly, while

Diego, to his surprise, was wide awake and focused on his phone. The screen was shattered, refusing to come on, but he kept on pressing the power button, relentlessly trying to get it on. "What the hell? When did this even happen?"

"Probably when you fell." Diego looked up at him. "I'll get you a new one when—"

"No thanks." He didn't waste time in turning down the offer. "I'm not your kid, Nicholas. Not everything that happens to me is your responsibility."

This had been his exact complaint the night before, which made it awkward for Nicholas. He had been looking after Diego for over ten years, so it *was* his responsibility. At some point, he realized he had stopped living for himself and started living for Diego instead. Nonetheless, he wholeheartedly embraced this newfound purpose. His life was bleak, and there was not much he looked forward to, so that made it bearable. They used to be a lot closer and more open with each other, but then things suddenly changed. Or rather, Diego had changed. He kept to himself more, avoiding Nicholas like the plague, taking it upon himself to do whatever he wanted. Despite how much Nicholas insisted he go to college and get a more useful degree, unlike him, Diego still went ahead, becoming an aircraft mechanic and enlisting in the military. He packed out of the apartment Nicholas had spent more than half of his annual salary to rent for both of them and moved to the McGuire dorms.

For Nicholas, it was as if he no longer knew how to talk to him. He had never felt their four-year age gap until then. It was like he only knew all the wrong words and did all the wrong things. It was really taking a toll on him.

He assumed that their 'conversation' had ended, so was shocked when Diego spoke to him. "How are you feeling now?"

Almost stuttering over his words, Nicholas quickly replied, "I should be the one asking you that, not the other way around."

"I'm not the one who got done in by a zombie."

"Fair point," he laughed awkwardly. "I'm alright. Or at least I think so. My stomach hurts, but every other part of me feels fine. Plus, from what I know, the effect is almost immediate. If nothing happened to me right after, then I doubt anything's going to happen at all. I'm okay; no need to worry."

"I'm not worried," Diego deadpanned. "To be honest, I won't be surprised if the effect doesn't work on you. It won't be the first time. With everything they did to you at the lab, there's no way your body is normal."

'The lab' he was referring to was where they had met several years ago, along with many others that had also been kidnapped. They seldom spoke of it, as it was a sensitive topic, but Diego must have felt comfortable enough to bring it up.

Nicholas, on the other hand, didn't want to think about it. "I doubt that's the reason," he said offhandedly.

"Nicholas, if everyone else who got attacked but you are turning into zombies, then there is no other reason."

Before they escaped, Nicholas had been at the lab the longest—more than four years—meaning he had suffered the most. Everyone who had been brought in at the same time as him, the children as well, had long since died. If not because of the cruel experiments conducted on them, then from the equally cruel living conditions. Many others that came later experienced the same fate.

The only reason Nicholas had survived that long was because of his markedly unique genetic constitution, which made him the most suitable for their sanguinary testing. He had been the preferred lab rat for the scientists before they eventually cast him aside.

With the number of things injected into him during that period, the idea that he was resistant to the effects of the Covid Prime virus was not far-fetched. Still, Nicholas didn't want to accept that that suddenly made him special. To him, the only thing those experiments had made him was worthless. His life had been ruined from the day he was hijacked from his parents and trafficked to Guam. He wanted nothing more to do with his ugly past.

Nicholas felt a random urge to pee, which granted him the perfect opportunity to evade the conversation. By the time he returned from the urinals, Josue had woken up as well.

"*Meu amigo*," He croaked out. "I'm starving. You know, I might just turn into a zombie and devour you all," Josue joked to the reception of cold glances; it occurred to him that his joke would have been a lot more appreciated had it not been frighteningly possible.

"Too soon, Josue, too soon." Nicholas shook his head. "Drink water. We're all hungry, but there's nothing we can do about that till tomorrow."

"It's quiet enough, I can risk it!"

"Have fun."

Nicholas sat back down in his sidewall seat and tuned out Josue's whining. He was drawing up a plan in his mind for their movements the next morning. He would go out at blue hour to confirm that it was safe for them to leave, then they would all escape from there before the sun rose.

He hoped that nothing had happened to his truck since that was what he would use to take both him and Diego home. The JB MDL would probably be shut down for a while, maybe forever. Nicholas honestly didn't see a way they could bounce back from this tragedy as he was sure they had sustained far too many casualties. He wondered if anyone else had survived like they had and were probably hiding about the base too. He would see on their way home, though he doubted it would matter; his immediate priority was Diego's safety, then his own. Either way, he was most likely out of a job. For some reason, that didn't bother him as much as he thought it would.

It felt like his plan was missing something. Then it dawned on him. He forgot about his father. Although Nicholas's relationship with his father was practically nonexistent, it had barely developed since they reunited a year and a half ago, he still felt obligated to make sure the old man, along with his wife and kid, were safe. He realized he would have to drive down to Hamilton to confirm that. He couldn't call him since he didn't have his number. He had never saved it because he couldn't imagine saving his contact as 'Dad' or the like. His father was his only biological relative but had contributed little to nothing to his life, even before his tragedy.

"Josue," Nicholas interrupted the other's lamenting, "where are you headed tomorrow after we get out of here?"

Josue looked at him like he had just asked him what his name was. "I was planning on going wherever you guys went." He stated so matter-of-factly that Nicholas's brow rose. "I live on the base, and my entire family is in Cali. I don't have anywhere else to go."

Nicholas ran a hand across his face, thinking about how he had to add Josue into the equation. His apartment was barely big enough for three of them, but it would do, and he didn't mind, much. After all, Josue had proven himself reliable enough to have around, though Nicholas would rather not admit it to him. "That's no problem, but are you planning on going back to California? Have you checked on your family members?"

"*No.* The thought of calling and nobody answering because they're all dead is too much for me." Josue's voice shook slightly as he spoke. "I'd rather go see them in person, although I don't know how possible that will be."

Nicholas didn't exactly have much of a family to think about, so he couldn't imagine the turmoil Josue was going through. He left it at that and turned to face Diego.

"The base has been compromised and is no longer a safe place to be. I think it's best you come with me." Diego only nodded, which was still a much better response than he had expected.

He had managed to come up with a rough plan; its success then depended on how things went the next day. Nicholas was not one for fate, but there and then, he found himself begging it to be in their favor come morning.

"Nicholas, it is weird that you haven't turned yet." Josue peered at him from his position on the floor. "I can almost swear the others I saw turned immediately. Plus, that's how it works in almost every zombie movie."

Nicholas didn't like where this was leading. He was not looking forward to part two of his talk with Diego. "I guess I'm just different," he said slowly.

"Then, is there a way you could stop others from turning too? Imagine if all we needed was an ounce of your blood to do the trick."

Nicholas frowned, but he knew that Josue was just having harmless fun with his theories, his little way of coping with the nightmare they had found themselves in, so he tried to evade the conversation as calmly as he could, despite his annoyance. He was sure his smile looked fake, but he plastered it on regardless. "I'd like not to think so."

"But what if?" Josue persisted. "It might not be your blood, but what if you were, like, the key? That would be so cool. Imagine having the power to save this fucked up world."

"Sergeant Franco," Diego said suddenly, causing them to look at him. He had been quiet that whole time, so they naturally paid him a lot of attention. "If I may, sir. I don't think that would be fun for anybody. Imagine the weight of the world on your shoulders. It doesn't sound very pleasant, does it now?"

Maybe he had noticed how uncomfortable Nicholas had been, or maybe he was just speaking his mind. Whatever the reason, Nicholas was immensely grateful for his interjection.

Josue scratched at his beard as he ruminated over those words. "You're right. I guess I got over-excited at the idea." He fell to his back and sighed. "I'm just a bit tired of everything at this point. It only gets worse and worse, like there's nothing to hope for anymore. I don't even know how to save myself from these feelings, so if somebody else could, then…" He left his words to hang in the air, never finishing his sentence.

Truthfully, they didn't need him to. They knew exactly what he felt because they felt the same way too; they just didn't have the confidence to say it out loud.

CHAPTER FOUR

KAREN

A somber mood had settled upon them this time, one that could not be broken. Nicholas didn't want to use his phone since he didn't know when he would be able to charge it if their plans fell through. He was learning to be wiser as time went by. Looking around him restlessly, as though a clue would present itself, he tried to figure out what to do next, but there was nothing else for him to do.

Reluctantly, he laid back and stretched, then closed his eyes and allowed himself to drift into an almost sound slumber again. This time around, things were different. He dreamt about his past. Memories he thought he'd repressed of the time he spent, aged twelve, caged like a wild animal in the torture room of a lab, where mad scientists had locked him up, punishment for all the stubborn kids who so much as dared to defy them.

It was a horrible place where monsters called 'humans' performed terrifying and inhumane experiments on him and all the other unfortunate children they had stolen from across the globe under the false banner of finding a cure. It was a memory Nicholas had long suppressed. Yet, the trauma from the zombies' onslaught had caused it to bubble up into his unconscious, sullying his fantasy world, aiming to cause him more harm and leave him more miserable than he already was.

He remembered how it felt to be chained to the white walls and starving for days as if he was still crawled up in a corner, pleading for death to release him once more. For almost a week, they had abandoned him there, not even coming to release him once or check up on him, but he was pretty sure they were watching, tracking him.

He spent the first couple of days that passed crying and sobbing gently. The next succeeding days, he would yell and shout at the top of his voice just to get their attention, but all proved to no avail. They were satisfied with knowing he was alive; his wellbeing was none of their concern. Soon his clothes were reduced to nothing more than filthy rags that barely hung onto his sickly frame as he soiled himself day in and day out until he felt his stench and filth would suffocate him. When they did manage to feed him, they set the food tray a good distance away, taking pleasure in watching him strain and tug along his heavy chains to get to it. At times when the fatigue was too much, he'd simply give in to despair and starve himself rather than struggle for his food, but the scientists would not let him die. Though he struggled to drink the water he was given it once in a while.

The lab was designed to mess with the psychology of all those who ever stepped foot into it. Its scientists went out of their way to emotionally destabilize their patients; they saw the children in their care as nothing more than disposable pawns.

The only thought he could remember entertaining rather than death was escaping the treacherous lab. He had a fever and slipped in and out of consciousness regularly, and even with that, no one came in to check up on him; if their conditions were not deemed severe, then they were left to wallow in their filth and pain. Nicholas might have been young, but even he knew he was on the verge of death. He would wish for it to claim him that instant, whenever he was awake. He had struggled to survive for so long that, ironically, he no longer wanted to live.

Even with all of the hardships he faced, suicide was never an option for him, apart from the fact that the scientist would always intervene just in time to save him. He knew he could have easily used the chains to strangle himself before they had realized it, or he could have been resourceful and devised some other way to end himself more peacefully, but for some reason, he never did. He had lost hope on the thought of escape, yet he could not bring himself to end it all and instead bore through the hell that had become his life.

There were times when the medications they did give him left him delirious enough to hallucinate and talk to himself. Even when he was not under the influence of some drug or the other, he would see things that weren't there and act on his delusional impulses like a nutjob.

By the third week, when his expectations of death grew stronger, the head of the illegal research group finally came in its stead. His name was Dr. Actassi, but they called him *father*. Their numbers had dropped drastically. Nicholas had not met the others initially, but from their cries, he could tell there were hundreds of them within the tiny cells where they always lay, chained to the wall, till the scientists saw the need for them. By the time Dr. Actassi took over their supervision, the hundreds of voices had reduced to a few inaudible moans and muffled cries. The three weeks they had been starved and drugged had served as a sort of test where they weeded out those without the mental fortitude to persevere. Hundreds of children died, and soon there was barely even a handful of their original number. If Nicholas had known that the worst was yet to come, then maybe he would have killed himself earlier, as so many other children did.

He always wondered why the doctor liked to be called *father* but never seemed to come to the knowledge of it—he was too busy trying to get away to care. Being the head of the research couldn't have been the straight-up reason for being called *father*. 'Go. We have no use for you, *no*,' Dr. Actassi always said with a cold and owlishly haunting tone as he kicked over a plate of food with a devious smirk on his face.

Nicholas remembered that he had always spoken to them with much affection even though he treated them as savages. How could a human be built like that? How could he treat his fellow humans like they were some animals? In his eyes, it was almost as if they were not humans but the lowliest of animals, maybe not even worthy of being called living beings.

Contrary to his words, father didn't unchain him, but he made sure to kick the food close enough for Nicholas to strain his neck and devour it like a dog. 'Go. We have no use for you, *no*,' he repeated coldly. The words echoed in the empty lab until it became the only thing he could hear, tearing through his eardrum and deafening him. He could see them written in the air, written everywhere in sight. They floated over to him and wrapped around his neck, squeezing harder and harder. He choked on nothing and writhed in agony as his vision became enveloped in darkness. He was dying. He was finally dying.

Nicholas's eyes flew open as he jumped up in his seat. His breathing was ragged, and he was soaked in a cold sweat. He had to blink several times before registering that he was awake and no longer in that dreadful lab. It took him almost twenty minutes to shake off the haunting feeling that had accompanied him from his dreams, but he eventually calmed down. Although he had long since been diagnosed with Post-Traumatic Stress Disorder, it had been a while since he last had a nightmare like that. He blamed it on his earlier conversation with the others rather than the zombies beyond the hangar, more than eager to make a meal of them.

Nicholas glanced about worriedly to learn that the others were still fast asleep, unfazed by his sudden outburst. Soundlessly, he rose to his feet, walked over to where Josue had dumped his backpack earlier, and fished out another water bottle. He downed its contents in mere seconds, feeling as thirsty as a marathon runner probably would by the end of his run.

Nicholas plopped back to the ground and sighed deeply, feeling relieved after he had grasped it was all a dream. He brought out his phone and saw that it was already half-past five. The time had come. The night had passed quietly and quickly, and he had higher hopes for their survival. The rest of the group also had faith in their survival, but Nicholas could bet more.

He got up and searched for his full-body suit but changed his mind when he saw how banged up it was. It looked really terrible. That was when he realized that he looked a mess. Examining himself, he was surprised at how long he had gone without noticing how messed up he looked. He probably smelled like one of those things too, although his nose had become acquainted with his stink. He tiptoed towards the tap so that he wouldn't wake anyone from their peaceful sleep, wanting to clean himself up a bit. He washed his face quietly and then struggled to remove the dried goo from his rough hair. Nicholas felt he was ready after he had rinsed out most of it. It was all he could do.

Having cleaned himself up the best he could, he went back into the fuselage to find his wrench, his Glock, and the crowbar. The rivet gun was still in his holster, and he tucked his gun in it too. Whenever his hand went down to his holster, and he felt the presence of his weapon, he always felt secure and safe.

While he was doing his best not to make a lot of noise, he pulled down the door he had entered through and exited the plane silently. Nicholas gave himself a moment to adjust to the nightlight, his pupils expanding, before he continued down the steps. He made every move with much caution, eyes darting left and right to fully capture the situation. By the time he got to the entrance of the hangar, he confirmed that he had no other company than bones, rotten corpses, and himself. The bones, rotten corpses, and the likes were scenes he was getting used to seeing.

Although the stench of the dead was so heavy that it made his stomach turn, the chilly wind that whipped at him when he stepped outside was almost heavenly. It had indeed been hell inside the Hercules, and being outdoors, he wished he would not have to go back inside, even though he knew that was not plausible. Nicholas looked around, but there was not a single soul in sight. At least not one that he spotted. He walked further down the flight line, all the way past the 305th Squadron, and still didn't see anybody. The oppressive silence was almost unbearable. He just wished he could yell names as loud as he could.

It seemed that the coast was clear, so he turned back and quickly returned to the 905th's hangar. When he walked in, one of them desperately needed to shower before they moved.

Diego's ankle didn't hurt as much as before, and he could put more pressure on it. Walking was hard, but he managed. The other two remained at his side to support him if he needed any help until they got to Nicholas's truck. The sight of his Toyota Tacoma in excellent condition (other than the goo and blood stains) set Nicholas's heart at total ease. Finally, there was something that didn't look gross or messy. They all got in the truck.

At first, he couldn't find the keys in his pocket. Frustration had already set in when the key was spotted on the mat in his driver's seat. Quickly, he put in the key, reviving the engine effortlessly with just one turn. Nicholas flicked on his headlights which shone brightly in the morning's darkness, and drove off, carefully monitoring the road before him in preparation for any sudden attacks. The entire base was in a wretched state, tainted with traces of despair and destruction. The grounds were bathed in the blood and guts of both the dead and undead. Usually, everything would look crazy, but after the last 24 hours, it all looked normal to them. There were many indicators of fires and fierce combat, the shells of bullets, shot in vain, were scattered about. Cars that collided with each other could also be spotted, some of them still burning, lighting up the morning a little.

They felt less miserable when they came across other survivors further down. Although they were few in number, all the same, they were still thankful. Nicholas stopped so that they could each exchange one or two words with those they recognized. It was as if there was an unspoken agreement between them and their colleagues to keep their shared horror stories short. In all his years of working at the joint base, Nicholas had yet to bond with anybody, but he was certain that his eyes mirrored the haunted look in theirs. The unspeakable events they had all witnessed and experienced the day before would bind them together in eternal trauma.

They left at dawn. They didn't see any signs of a hoard for a short part of the drive, but they knew it was too good to be true. Every corner should've been crawling with them by then. The outside world was practically identical to the JB MDL, with remnants of corpses strewn everywhere they passed. It was as if the earth had been painted scarlet. Once they drove off the McGuire Boulevard onto the bloody road, some greenish-gray zombies appeared in the distance. They looked far gone, eyes dead and body decayed like they could fall apart in an instant. Initially, there were just three or four moving about aimlessly, twisting and turning their heads involuntarily, with their hands out in front. Then, without any warning, they drastically multiplied tenfold.

Nicholas tightened his grip on the wheel as his heart began to raise. "You guys' better belt up. We are going for a bumpy ride." The next moment, he slammed his foot on the accelerator, and they bolted forward, plundering through the hoard which had gathered around the outskirts of Wrightstown. Only a few of the swarm's missing zombies could save them. Otherwise, their truck might have become stranded amid the crowd.

There was not a single human being in sight, at least none that were alive. A few of them were already injured and infected but still evolving. Those who were unfortunate enough to be caught outside were already dead meat.

Despite the power and speed of the truck, which he had enhanced with his throttle controller, forcing his way through was no easy feat. There were other vehicles that were parked on the roads, and because he couldn't do much to avoid the zombies, climbing over the tons he knocked down, it slowed him down considerably.

"Shit." Nicholas could see more of them in the distance, and by the looks of it, they wouldn't make it through the gathering hoard that wasn't far off. They had probably swarmed the whole town. He could only imagine how much worse the capital would be. Terrible. Jessica's face flashed in his mind, and he gritted his teeth. No matter what, he still had to go.

"Diego, Josue. I'll give you the keys to my apartment and drop you off in front."

"And then what happens to you?" Diego snapped at him from behind, half dazed. He had been having a tough time adjusting to everything. He was at the height of his nerves, and this was not helping.

"I'm going straight to Trenton after, but I'll be fine on my own."

"Why? Do you have family there?" Josue gave him a puzzled look from across the passenger seat.

"Something like that," Nicholas said over the sound of flesh splattering and bones crunching under his tires as he swerved onto the street before his.

"Are you for real right now?" Diego yelled. "They've taken over Wrightstown, but you still want to carry yourself to the freakin' capital! If you go any further, you're going to get trapped by the hoard!"

"As long as you're both safe, it's a risk I don't mind taking," he said so calmly it pissed off Diego more. He hated this side of Nicholas. It always made him feel as if he were arguing with a wall, and went silent in anger.

Nicholas turned onto his street, which was thankfully less populated with zombies than the ones before. Their numbers had diminished slightly on the way here. He was about to park in the driveway of his apartment building when Josue stuck out his hand and blocked the steering wheel.

"Sergeant—"

"Sergeant Sims."

Nicholas quietened immediately. This was the first time Josue had ever addressed him this way, so whatever he had to say was serious.

Josue was emotional already. "It's possible that I'm speaking too soon. You very recently began treating me as if I didn't exist." He chuckled. "But even if I don't have the authority, I'll say it. You aren't alone; therefore, you don't have to confront every challenge independently. Aren't we now Wingmen, pals, Nicholas? At least, that is how I feel. Diego, I'm sure, feels the same way."

Nicholas strummed his fingers on the dashboard for a few seconds, thinking, before he let out a sigh. Why couldn't they understand that he just didn't want to trouble them? The zombies, sensing their presence, had turned their deformed heads in their direction and were trudging towards them menacingly. There was no time left to waste, and he didn't have the strength for further conversation.

"I hope I don't regret this," Nicholas said swiftly, almost in a whisper, then adjusted the brake and swiftly reversed out of the drive, ramming into the zombies behind him. Fearing they would climb into the back of the truck, he turned as fast as he could and sped off down the street. Luckily, they were all saved, the zombies were not able to climb up the back of the truck.

Diego said nothing while Josue pumped his fist in the air in excitement, feeling happy. He made it out of the troubles alive.

Nicholas wondered why on earth he would be excited to go on a death trip, but he decided to just focus on the journey ahead instead of overthinking it. He drove at the fastest speed that would not kill them as the crunching underneath his tires grew louder. Since he had gotten used to it, navigating through the zombies felt easier, but he had to be careful so that they had no opportunity to climb into the truck or jump on his windscreen. It would probably be the end of them if the zombies were successful in breaking it or any window at all.

The sun rose, and the environment became serene as they traveled the roads connecting to the capital. With the hoard thinning out, the sunlight exposed the whole event of the night. Everything could be seen clearly. The burning cars, the dead humans, the crushed zombies, the blood-filled roads, even the spilled guts of the dead were all over the place. As if suddenly thrust into an alternate world, that changed the moment they entered Trenton territory. Everywhere you looked, there were people, and then there were zombies. Their collective growls, as they devoured, formed an angry buzz over their heads.

Nicholas kept his foot on the accelerator without thinking twice, but the deeper they dived into the madness, the thicker the hoard became. They were getting slowed down by the huge mass in front of them. As they edged closer to Hamilton, zombies occupied almost every other space than the one his truck took up, and it was becoming increasingly difficult to pave their way through. The truck's initial speed had reduced slowly, almost getting stopped by the crowd around it. The other two didn't make a single sound of complaint throughout, but he could see the fear in their eyes.

Somehow, almost like he was dragging the truck along, they managed to turn onto White Horse Avenue, and he forced his way down to where his father's largely built one-story ranch house was located.

"There's no point in all of us getting down. I'll go in first, and that's non-debatable. Call if you need help, and I'll do the same if anything happens." He glanced at Josue, hesitating for a moment. "Since Diego's phone is broken, I'll call you, so be on standby. Okay?"

Josue nodded, repeatedly concurring with what he was told.

Nicholas parked in front of the house and quickly unbuckled his seatbelt. He looked around. The majority of zombies on the street were focused on assaulting and ravaging the people who had made the mistake of stepping outside. Their victims had tried to fight back, even some of those indoors, but it was futile. The heavy blast of shotguns only attracted them, and the bullets dismembered them at most.

Although focused on their current prey, a few had already fixed their empty gaze on the truck, having sensed it when it crept in, even though Nicholas tried to drive in quietly. Nicholas stretched his hand to the backseat to drag his mechanic overalls to him. Thinking it would be better to wear something that would leave his skin unexposed, he struggled into it. He felt opening the door was risky, so he pushed the button for the sunroof.

Diego eyed him nervously, worried about his size. "Can you fit?"

"We'll see."

The glass above slid fully open, and he pushed his arms through, placing his hands on the outer roof. Nicholas was slim and muscular enough, plus it was wide, so he didn't think there would be a problem. He pulled himself up until half of him had passed through, then crawled out, standing up as slowly and as noiselessly as he could. Once he had carefully balanced himself on the roof of the Tacoma, he had Josue pass him his usual weapons.

"Nicholas," Diego called out as Josue pressed the button for the sunroof. "Do what you need to do and fast, then let's get the hell out of here and go home. Please—"

The glass slid shut, cutting off his voice, but his words had reached Nicholas nonetheless, who had gotten the message. Wrench in one hand and crowbar in the other, he jumped down onto the drive silently with a bobcat's agility, swinging his arms at the two zombies that had shuffled close enough for him to take them out effortlessly. They fell back, dazed and confused, while Nicholas landed on his feet. It took the zombies only a moment to regain their bearing, moving closer to attack him once again. He swung his wrench forward and hit the first on the head, making it fall into the other, knocking them to the ground, along with its dislocated jaw.

Immediately bursting into a sprint, Nicholas ran down the lawn like a driven mad man towards the porch of their home, knocking down anything that approached him. There were fewer zombies in his path as most of them were too distracted by the boom of gunshots that continued to erupt in the distance as he ran right past the few in his way. The shouts and wails of people terrified and fighting for their lives out of his sight, as awful as it was, worked to his benefit, making it increasingly harder for most zombies to pay attention to him.

He had just darted up the steps when he heard someone scream from inside. Despite its heightened, fearful pitch, he could easily detect to whom it belonged. It sounded like the shrill voice of a teenage girl, which made him panic and shiver, hoping nothing had happened to her. Nicholas knew that if he bashed a window or carelessly broke down the door, it would come to bite him in the ass later, but he didn't know how else to deal with the smart lock. The last time he was there, he had not seen the need to ask for the code or how it worked because he never planned on returning. He stared at it exasperated, and it unexpectedly beeped and flashed green. He was stunned when he heard a couple of clicks, and the door was blown open a bit by the wind. He just stood there and stared at the open door, speechless.

What the hell?

He decided to leave it at that and pushed the door back. Nicholas stepped into the elegantly styled living room and saw that it was devoid of any occupants. He was thinking of where to go next when he heard another scream and a young blonde-haired girl of about fifteen came running from the other end of the room.

"Jessica!" He cried out, rushing forward.

His half-sister whipped her head to the side, and her distraught eyes fell on him, widening in confusion. Physically, she appeared to be fully alive and fine too, without any infections. But those crystal orbs were brimming with tears as she just about collapsed in Nicholas's arms out of mixed emotions.

"Why's this happening?" she asked him amidst the tears. Despite her shock at his sudden appearance, she clung to him, shaking terribly.

"It's okay. It's okay," he cooed as he released everything he was holding so he could embrace her properly. "What's wrong? Where are your mom and dad? Are you the only one home?"

She shook her head violently, hiccupping as she spoke, "They're in the kitchen…but Mom…."

Something had clearly happened to his stepmom, Karen. He hoisted Jessica up into his arms and carried her to a sofa, settling her down gently in a position that would allow her to breathe properly. He ran his hand through her hair in a bid to calm her down, but she suddenly hit his chest, trying to push him back.

"You have to go now! Just please save Dad!"

He was shocked by her reaction, but he enclosed those hands in his, squeezing tightly. "Take it easy and tell me what's going on."

Jessica blinked at him through the tears, then took a deep breath.

"Mom…Dad told Mom not to go out because of the virus thing, but Mom… didn't listen. She went to the supermarket without telling us, but we assumed things were still fine when she came back." She sounded small, like she was much younger, just a fragile little child. "Then she started acting really weird, and then…and then she started attacking

Dad…so he told me to run, and I think he locked both of them inside the kitchen," She explained as tears flowed from her eyes.

Nicholas schooled his expression, stopping himself from reacting in a way that would upset her any further, but within his mind, he knew that it was too late. Karen had obviously turned into a zombie, and his dad, who had decided to sacrifice himself, would soon follow suit. How could he tell her that even though they were just a breath away, she had lost her parents?

Jessica had survived in their place, and the best Nicholas could do was ensure her safety. He was thinking about how to get her to the truck when she tugged on his arm. "Please, before me, save Dad. He's still okay." She couldn't even look him in the eye but said it again and again as a broken record stuck on a loop.

Her voice broke, and Nicholas felt a soft twinge in his heart. She refused to let him go until he breathed out a yes. He gripped her shoulders before she could fall back onto the couch. "I might not be able to save him, but I will bring him back to you."

Jessica's lips trembled, but she forced herself to smile. It was awkward, but Nicholas understood it was the most genuine way she could express her gratitude at that moment. It didn't matter whether or not they lacked that special brother-sister bond, it hurt him to see her that way.

"Go and stay in the guest's washroom. If anything happens to you, scream as loud as you can, and I'll come running." He followed her into the room, making sure where she had hidden was actually safe before he left her side.

Walking past the dining room, he headed to the kitchen, approaching it cautiously, his weapons in hand. He gripped onto them like holding them was holding his life. He could already hear his stepmom's ravenous snarling from some meters away. He turned the door handle silently, confirming that the door was locked.

Nicholas was going to have to go in with a bang. He knew the implications of what he was about to do and hesitated a little before shaking the thoughts from his head. Taking several steps back, he twisted himself slightly so that his shoulder jutted forward, then rushed at the kitchen door. He threw himself at it with all his might, and it gave way, flying open.

His sudden intrusion did the job of attracting Karen's attention, just like he had expected. She immediately shifted her focus from his father, who got hit by the door and was slammed against one of the shelves, to Nicholas, who took in her disheveled appearance. Her skin was cracked and visibly rotting, peeling off in multiple places. He felt sorry for his stepmom. Some of the skin on her face was also gone, revealing her sunken cheekbones. The cool, pretentious look her blue eyes had always reflected at him had been replaced by a vicious, yellow-tinted glare. She looked just about ready to devour him even though she had a big lump of flesh trapped between her teeth.

That flesh was the missing chunk of his father's right thigh, from which blood gushed out profusely. He held onto his half-destroyed leg as he slumped to the floor and groaned in pain, looking at his son, who had just randomly shown up, with much bewilderment. It was as if he didn't know what other expression to put on, feeling so many things at the same time. Nicholas knew because he felt the same way, but he had jumped in headfirst into this messed up family situation ignoring that.

"Phillip!" he shouted at his father as Zombie Karen snatched at him. The last time he called him 'Dad' was when he was eight. "I'll explain later, just close your eyes for now." Of course, he could still hear them, but Nicholas didn't want his father to witness the fight that was about to ensue and was glad that the old man weakly did as he said. Obeying quietly, he turned around, writhing in pain.

Nicholas spun the wrench, whacking it against Karen's waist, whispering an apology as he did so. She knocked against the kitchen counter but snapped back up and lunged at him again. The kitchen was rather spacious, but having to be conscious of his father in the corner, keeping him away from Karen's claws, made moving about hard for him. Nicholas managed to dodge, and she hit the fridge instead. The handle flew at him, missing by just a split second as he swiped at it with his crowbar, flinging it elsewhere. He smacked her in the face with that same crowbar while simultaneously using the wrench to shank her in the stomach. There was a loud crack as her head swiveled to the side, but she twisted it back the next second, roaring at him. It pained Nicholas deeply that she was putting up a fight. It felt as though every blow he threw at her struck himself, and though he wished he could end it quickly, he knew not to be too hasty, or it would cost them all their lives.

He dug the wrench deeper into the hole it had created in her stomach, and her fresh congealed blood spilled out. Nicholas tried to duck as she reached for him, but she successfully grabbed onto his hair. Karen's grip was unimaginably strong, so strong it reminded him of the zombie that had damn near disemboweled him the previous day, but this time around, it felt as though she would pull his scalp clean off his body. He tried to hit her again with the crowbar, but she swung him so violently it fell out of his hand.

Disoriented on the kitchen floor with both his weapons knocked out of his reach, it appeared things had taken a turn for the worse. Zombie Karen was winning the fight. Kicking at her didn't work as she continued swinging him, unscathed by his futile attempts at defense, painfully pulling at his hair. She bashed him against the sink, and he hit his head hard against the tap. The impact knocked the handle clean off, and a burst of water came gushing out. Nicholas had gotten more than a bruise from the attack, with a bloody gash across his temple, when the flurry of water had him choking as it got in his nose and mouth. It stung as it splashed in his eyes and touched his wound. He was coughing and sputtering as she released her grip and flung him aside like a ragdoll.

Nicholas slammed against the bin, knocking it over, and hit the floor hard. He felt like every inch of his face and body was on fire, and he just kept crying out in pain. Was Zombie Karen still filled with enmity towards him because what the hell? She packed a punch for such a small woman who had just turned. Or maybe she was just hungry.

He couldn't open his eyes yet. Every time he tried, it stung, so he felt around blindly for his drill gun, fishing it out quickly, knowing it was loaded with bits and a battery already. Nicholas could sense that her footsteps had changed direction, which meant she had switched targets. With much struggle, he dragged himself up while trying to blink away the sharp pain in his eyes. She was just a few feet away from his father, so he had to act fast. He crept up behind her quietly and had her in a chokehold the next instant. She was half-dead, so it didn't have that much of an effect, but he didn't need it to. With his free hand, Nicholas held the drill gun to her head and pressed down on the trigger. It whirred to life, shooting forward, drilling a hole in the middle of her forehead and into her brain. She bellowed, and he released her, using that moment to pull his wrench out. He swung at her knees, and she fell to the ground. A familiar feeling of guilt flooded his heart as he raised his wrench in the air to deliver the finishing blow. Ironically, and sadly too, it was interlaced with a dangerous indifference because truth was Nicholas didn't care much for her. She had always treated him with a hidden hostility, so they never got along well, and here he was, about to kill her. It was a torturous feeling, but he had to do it in his father's stead.

He gritted his teeth. "Philip, please. Just, don't open your eyes," Nicholas pled as his wrench came crashing down on her skull, specifically aiming at the area he had already drilled through. Her head split open with a loud crack. He hit her again until the wrench was all the way in the pile of mush her brain had become. Particles spilled all over the kitchen floor, making it all messier as the purple-tinged red goo mixed in with all the water flooding the room. Panting heavily, Nicholas threw the wrench into the sink. It needed a serious wash.

He staggered to where his father was, stepping into the puddle of blood that encircled him. That was when he noticed that Karen had injured Philip in more than one place. There were big, dark red stains around his shoulder and right under his ribs where his shirt had been slashed. It was to be a pitiful end; he had been stripped of the chance to turn and was taken straight to death's door.

"Nicholas," Phillip mumbled as he crouched down in front of him, eyes still squeezed shut. "Are you okay? I hope she didn't infect you too."

The man was fatally wounded and was most definitely in indescribable suffering, yet he still had the strength to ask after his son, who had just murdered his wife. Despite the kind gesture, being on the receiving end of this affection only confounded Nicholas. He could never get used to the new, supposedly caring side of his father that had developed during the years they had been out of touch. The father he knew was cold-hearted and selfish, but then again, he was Jessica's father too, and Nicholas guessed that had changed things.

"Are you okay?" his feeble voice sounded again.

"You know I've been through worse. Even if she hurt me, Phillip, I've been attacked by them before. I don't get infected, don't worry. Just focus on breathing."

"I can tell I'm dying." He shook his head sadly. He finally opened his eyes, revealing the emeralds that had lost their glow. "There's no point. I'd rather die knowing you and Jessica are alive and safe." Nicholas nodded in the affirmative, and his father let out a shaky breath. "Thank you." Crimson tears rolled down his cheek. "I'm sorry, I couldn't bring myself to do it." He continued, "I'm sorry for putting you through that." His incessant apologies sounded so miserable, pathetic even, making Nicholas uncomfortable. "You say you've been through worse like it's nothing when I'm the one who put you through that. I neglected you, even on that day. It was my fault you got kidnapped. It's my fault your mother left, my fault you had to be alone for so long."

Nicholas couldn't take it anymore. "Phill—"

"You still gave me a second chance, yet all I've done is ruin your life. I'm a selfish bastard even in death, leaving Jessica to be your responsibility after I abandoned you for a new family. But if anything good can come out of all the horrible things I've done to you, then please…"

Nicholas begged him to stop talking when Phillip started coughing out blood, but he would not listen.

"If you can even save the world, then do it. You have to live your life now that I'm finally gone. A life without anything holding you back." He closed his eyes and leaned against the shelf. "I've wanted to say that for a while. I'm glad. There's something for Jessica hidden in one of the cabinets. Please give it to her." His voice sounded raw and weak, and his breath hitched as he coughed out more blood. "Thank you, Nicholas, for coming to find me. I'm sorry."

CHAPTER FIVE

SAVE THE WORLD

After his father took his last breath, Nicholas hesitated with a heavy heart. He couldn't imagine the look on Jessica's face if her late father were to stroll out of the kitchen and lunge at her, so he took the drill gun and drilled a hole clean through Philip's head before throwing a rag over his face.

"*Goodbye, father,*" Nicholas whispered to himself as he fought back the tears. They didn't deserve this. He was not fond of them, but they didn't deserve to lay in a puddle of gore in their final moments, sadly he didn't have the time to do anything about it. His sister, Jessica, needed him more than ever, so he did as he was told.

Once he had grabbed everything he needed, including the sealed box Phillip had requested he give Jessica, he returned to the living room. After getting most of the blood clean off his clothes and wounds, he hurried over to where Jessica had hidden, then swiftly began to pack her a bag so she'd go home with him. Nicholas made an effort to keep her from discovering her parents' bodies but soon realized that Jessica had already been avoiding the kitchen. She had heard it all happen; she didn't need to see the aftermath.

Before they left, Nicholas hesitated, still troubled by the thought of leaving their parents to rot on the kitchen floor. Jessica took his hand tightly, almost as though she'd read his mind.

"We can't leave them," Jessica finally voiced. "Not like *that.*"

"We can't bury them either." Nicholas frowned, hiding his gaze from her as he eyed the street for any sudden movements that would alarm them of any zombies nearby. Jessica squeezed something into his hand, and Nicholas paled, a grim expression of shock plastered across his face.

"We don't have to…" Jessica managed as Nicholas took the lighter from her, pulling her into a sad, awkward hug. Jessica understood that with the rate at which things were going, she had to be tough; it only surprised Nicholas that she would be the one to decide to burn the house, the home she had lived in all her life. Jessica had made a tough decision, and Nicholas was willing to see it through for both their sakes.

Nicholas had Jessica hide in the garage as he made his way back to the kitchen with a small can full of gasoline. The smell of iron and gore had begun to reek as he rummaged through the drawers for any and everything flammable he could get his hands on. After dousing the tabletops in whiskey and gasoline, he paused in the middle of the kitchen. The cloth he put over his father's face had soaked up blood and darkened, and what was left of Karen's head had drowned in the pool of water. The blood and gore triggered a wide range of emotions, dividing between sadness, remorse, and terror. Nicholas shook his head and steeled his resolve.

Pushing the last of his emotions aside, he spilled the fuel all over the rest of the house, from the hallway to the living room and other bedrooms, before stepping into the garage to walk Jessica to the front yard. Together they watched the light he lit outside follow a trail of gasoline back into the house. In a matter of seconds, the house was engulfed. Jessica refused to leave until the gas went off with a thunderous boom and the house was completely consumed; she was optimistic that her parents' remains would perish in the blaze.

Nicholas watched the house raze for a while as Jessica clung to him, sniffling as she fought back the tears though she was too stubborn to leave just yet. The implication pulled him in before he snapped out and decided to go back to what mattered. With Jessica by his side, he had no time to be distracted, though he hoped that when the carnage was all over, he'd finally allow himself to feel all the emotions he was supposed to.

He scowled as he looked down at his phone. He suspected that the other two outside were in danger, based on the number of missed calls he'd received from Josue, but he knew that his truck was the most at risk of being destroyed by the zombies. To his luck, the garage had a car in it, an SUV, his father's favorite. On his way out, he took the keys from a counter and drove away.

Just as he had feared, right around the block, he saw Diego and Josue huddled in the backseat of his truck, fighting against a horde of zombies that had been ceaselessly clawing at the car to get to them. The zombies, although slow in movement, acted as though they were crazed, controlled by one single force. Revving into sight, his engine's roaring over the sound of a struggle, he managed to draw some of the zombie's attention. Immediately shifting towards his direction, they came at the car, with a un quenching lust for blood.

They were still inside the Tacoma despite the fact that the zombies had bashed in its windows, even the windscreen, in a bid to secure their next meal. When Josue saw Nicholas thundering towards the truck in an SUV, he forcefully flung the door open—knocking some zombies over—and he and Diego jumped out. They quickly ran into the car, which had come to a stop right before them, and Nicholas took off.

As he drove through the stampede of zombies that threatened to upturn the car, he refused to stop or go slow. The vehicle hit quite a number of zombies, decapitating them while trying to get to the truck, and the further it drove through the zombie swamp, the more blood and gore increasingly coated the vehicle's exterior.

Nicholas continued to bulldoze through the horde, and by the time he connected to the highway leading back to Wrightstown, their numbers had greatly reduced. The ramp was free of traffic, though it was a rough drive, with several vehicles lying across the street like barricades because their owners had abandoned them in a hurry, fleeing for safety, but it was a safe drive. The zombies seemed to be fewer on the abandoned highway, probably because no one dared to use the road after the first hordes came through town or were drawn away by those who had fled. They did encounter a pair or two, but never enough to count as a mob or pose a threat to their vehicle as they cautiously maneuvered through traffic.

They made it to Nicholas's apartment building without any further events. A quick escape would have been to their advantage, but they couldn't risk a zombie managing to get into their SUV if they left it simply lying in the driveway. Nicholas found a significant rag tucked away in the trunk, and with Josue's help, they managed to camouflage their vehicle amongst the trees a short walk away from their place. Diego would have preferred they drove up to the apartment, but Josue clearly stated that the car would only draw more attention than they could handle.

Jessica had fallen asleep during the drive; it was not until they had finally managed to find a hiding spot for the car that they realized she'd actually passed out. The young men couldn't blame her, be it the fatigue or the mental stress from the ordeal she had just been through; fact remained, they had to look after her.

"I'll carry her." Nicholas declared. The others frowned.

"I don't think you noticed, bud…" Josue protested, "but you look like shit."

He felt like it too. The sharp pain at the side of his head, from when he got rammed into the sink, had gone, but in its place remained a throbbing headache. Nicholas would not admit it, but he feared he was severely concussed. It pained him that Josue had a point.

"You can't carry her…." Nicholas sighed "The building is probably crawling with zombies, and you're in better shape than I am."

"What exactly does that imply?" Diego smirked. He hadn't said it, but he didn't need to because his leg was still in intense pain. He was still as agile as ever, but he was in no condition for a battle if the necessity came, as Nicholas and Josue had noticed.

"If things go south, we might have to fight our way to the elevator, and Josue's our zombie expert," Nicholas rebuffed to his brother's annoyance.

Diego let out an exasperated sigh that startled Nicholas and Josue. "We ain't got time for this," he snapped as he heaved Jessica onto his back. Diego didn't have a problem with her weight, but his ankle screamed under him the moment she got on his back.

"I'm fine," Diego barked at the worried look Nicholas and Josue were giving him. "Now, just lead the damn way—" A thud in the distance cut off his reply. If there weren't any zombies in the area, then zombies are on there way.

A small group of five or six shuffled down the street. Josue's eyes widened with shock when one of them in particular caught his eye. To the forefront of the mindless horde stood a lanky zombie in what used to be a white shirt and bowtie—a zombie they had missed by an inch while making their drive to Nicholas's apartment. "That bloody zombie followed us," Josue gasped awkwardly; his reaction had an undertone of excitement that managed to put off Nicholas and Diego.

Enough had been said; Diego had a point, they couldn't afford to waste any more time. He led their charge to the elevator while Nicholas and Josue followed behind with a wrench and a crowbar. A zombie caught up to them from behind, but Josue knocked its brains out with a double-handed swing at its temple with his wrench. There were two other zombies in the hallway, but they had not noticed them till they got to the elevator.

Diego and Nicholas sighed with relief when they got in the building and realized the power was still on. The elevator was on the fourth floor, and with the horde that had stalked them from the highway gaining on them, they couldn't help but break a cold sweat. Another zombie darted at Josue, but he slammed his wrench into its head so hard it got too wedged in for him to retrieve it. The elevator arrived with a ding.

Diego's eyes lit up with a grin right before the doors slid open, and yet another zombie lunged out of the bloody elevator at him. It felt as though his life flashed before his eyes; of course, his immediate priority was shielding Jessica, so it surprised him that as he fell back to the ground clutching her, the zombie didn't descend on him.

"Get in," Nicholas roared through gritted teeth as the zombie gnawed at his balled fist. Nicholas bit his tongue as he thrust his crowbar into the zombie's eye and out the other side of its head as it bit down on him. His hand hurt like hell as he pried the zombie's teeth out of it and hurried onto the elevator with Diego and the others. Once the elevator doors had closed and he was sure they had made it through the worst of it, he thanked the heavens that he had managed to get to them on time. He didn't know how they escaped the horror and terror outside in the city, but one thing he knew was that they made it somehow.

Diego stared at Nicholas, bewildered, as a myriad of thoughts berated him, but of course, they all circled to a single question. *Why did you do that?* The elevator was no place for a conversation; the floor was covered in gore, probably what was left of whoever was trapped in it with that zombie. They all stood in awkward silence as Josue caught his breath, and Nicholas painstakingly dug through his wound for teeth left behind by the zombie. No words needed to be said; they were all simply content with being alive.

Other than their ragged breaths and the electrical humming, the ascending elevator could have undoubtedly passed as empty. Upon getting to the fifth floor, Nicholas had never been happy to be heading back to his gloomy apartment. He and Diego were practically the only people on their floor, since most of the other apartments had not been rented out yet, so they weren't surprised to learn that their base was clear of any zombies.

Who would have known that Nicholas's lack of social life would pay off? Josue thought smugly to himself as they made their way to the front door.

Nicholas was sweaty, smelly, starving, and exhausted, all wrapped up with the throbbing pains in the pit of his stomach, hand, and head. Still, he entertained a swelling sense of delight at the minor victory they had just gotten. For all that he was in the moment, he was glad that they could all call themselves survivors. He had somehow managed through hordes of zombies—not unscathed—but alive.

Nicholas unlocked the front door for them, and Diego immediately dropped Jessica on the couch, with the utmost care, of course, before plopping onto the ground beside her like a limp log of wood. There was so much he wanted to say, but he was going through too much pain and figured resting his head a little first would do him a hell of a lot of good. Nicholas and Josue didn't seem to mind. They were really beat themselves as they rested, propped up against the door as if expecting a zombie to try and force their way in after them while they stood there.

Nicholas took a deep breath as he tended to his hand. He didn't think that in a day, he'd be mourning his father and caring for his half-sister all at once. It was just past ten in the morning, and though it felt like a lifetime had gone by, it was still correct of him to assume that that was probably the longest and worst day of their lives. Jessica had lost both of her parents in one day to the infection that struck as though it had made its way from hell, and she was obviously traumatized by it already. It was a miracle that she had managed to sleep through the struggle they had getting on the elevator, but she couldn't stay asleep forever, and though she was only just waking up, she looked just as exhausted as the rest of them. Nicholas insisted that she rest more comfortably in bed, which she did after helping herself to a tall glass of water. He was in dire need of a bath and some rest as well, so he busied himself with getting that ready, leaving Josue and Diego to sort out themselves.

While in the shower, Nicholas could clearly remember the peaceful expression his father had when he died in his arms. Then, he was haunted by the sound of the drill ripping through flesh as he saw to it that his father didn't join the zombies. Nicholas gagged, doubling over the drain as he felt vomit swell up inside him, yet he couldn't seem to get himself to throw up despite how much he retched. He remained frozen under the equally freezing shower coming down on his scar-ridden body. The water coming off was darkened by blood and dirt. What troubled him was the fact that most of the blood that dyed his bath crimson was not even his.

He never intended to entertain Josue's wild conspiracies, but after getting bitten downstairs and not being turned like everyone else by the time they got to his apartment, he was forced to accept the possibility that he was immune. Then another thought crossed his mind, one he had not had in an exceedingly long time, death. Nicholas didn't know why, but all of a sudden, he wondered if he would die in bliss one day. Did he deserve a peaceful death after the things he had done that day? Phillip's last words kept ringing hauntingly in his head. He comforted himself with the fact that he was simply doing what was needed to ensure his and his family's survival, yet he couldn't shake the thought off. How could he think of a blissful death when he couldn't even live a happy life?

Long before the zombies arrived, he'd already been a husk of himself, riddled with shame that would not allow him to so much as take off his shirt around his own brother. He rubbed one of his many shames on the side of his stomach, the memory of how he'd gotten it flashing vividly in his head as though it had been waiting on standby at the back of his mind. It was back in the lab when he was twelve. When the head of the illegal research, father, had asked him to leave, he was tired and weary from the chains, from being restrained, but despite being at death's door, he failed to win any sympathy from the monster. That was when father had kicked him so hard his shoe broke Nicholas's already weak and malnourished skin, which barely clung to his body. The thought of it made him cringe. He could remember how he had groaned in pain while father loomed over him in disgust.

He slowly dove back into reality; he survived before and was determined to stay especially because the lives hinging on his had doubled. The noise of rushing water finally snapped him from his trance, and he stopped trying to throw up and pulled himself back together again. The scars on his body would always remind him that he had survived hell once, and though that didn't necessarily mean he could move on, it meant he could do it again. Nicholas's past and the remnants of it that were etched onto his body haunted him terribly and would do so all his life.

His father's words echoed in his mind, '*If anything good...*'

For some reason, it made him think of what Josue said the previous night, but what good did him being resistant do? He knew that the effect of a lot of drugs and other chemicals didn't work on him, but he had no idea how that resistance could be built independently, and it was not something he could pass to or transfer on to others, not on his own at least. At the end of the day, he was useless, and it ate at him. Nicholas just wanted something that made him worthy of existing. It was frustrating that after an entire decade and more, he had nothing, not a family to turn to, not good memories to cherish, not even a career he could honestly boast of.

He came out of the bathroom, his head and heart hurting, with a towel around his waist. As he dressed and went back outside, he tried to suppress the intense self-hatred that had overcome him. Surprisingly, Diego had made pancakes for everybody; how a guy that could barely even stand a moment ago had managed to whip up pancakes made Nicholas question how long he had been in the shower.

"He would not shut up about it," Diego answered his unspoken question as he finally noticed the gust as Josue wolfed down pancake after pancake as though his life depended on it. *Of course, he wouldn't.* Nicholas sighed internally; it didn't come as a surprise to him. They were all starving.

"Grab a plate," Diego said. Nicholas obliged, taking a plate from the countertop and having Diego serve him a dozen poorly shaped pancakes. He was on the verge of asking for some syrup, but it dawned on him that not only was he too hungry to care, but he had also forgotten to get some from the supermarket a couple of days before the shit storm. He munched at the pancakes hungrily, just like Josue, when he noticed Jessica was not at the table.

"She already had hers and went back to sleep," Diego said as he noticed Nicholas's shifting eyes.

"Oh... she must be exhausted," Nicholas said flatly as he tried to eat his meal.

They all sat silently in the living room as they ate, their holographic television buzzing to life in front of them thanks to the electricity, but none of the channels would come on. It was almost as if they hadn't just survived a series of near-death experiences, save from the disturbing static from their television and the strange vibe of the apartment.

No one spoke too; they didn't need to. Somehow Josue had finally learned how to read a room, or he was just too exhausted to be his usual chatty self, so they all just sat down calmly, reminiscing about what had happened. The outbreak. The infection. Help. No one knew if a cure would ever be found to the sudden zombie crisis or how long they had before being driven out to get more supplies, or worse, the zombies found them. The only reasonable thing they could think of was their survival. How were they supposed to survive this vicious world filled with bloodthirsty zombies?

It was a miracle that one of the channels still managed to be up. It was a popular news network run by a home-based journalist, who apparently still had time to be on air regardless of the zombie onslaught. The show was not as neat and flashy as it usually was, but they could tell that whoever was on the other side of the screen had put in an effort to make things look as though all hell had not broken loose about them.

Neither Nicholas nor his companions were one for news, but they found themselves hanging onto every word she eloquently uttered. She spoke with an almost unnerving composure of the tragic news of the President, along with many other members of Congress and several other influential political figures who had fallen to the zombie attack. They weren't expecting news of rainbows and cupcakes, but once they had heard that, they were frozen by grim despair that they never thought possible.

"What the fuck did she just say—" Josue nearly screamed loud enough to wake the dead that had not already awoken had Nicholas not hit him in time.

"The *President*?" Jessica stirred.

Her already pale skin seemed to whiten even more at the horrible revelation. She couldn't seem to fall back asleep after eating, and the news scared the drowsiness out of her eyes. The President and several others within the white house had been lost to the virus. Also, according to the report, the Vice President's whereabouts remained unknown to the public as he had been lost in all the carnage when hordes of zombies overran the White House. With nobody on the seat and both the ruling and opposition parties practically wiped out by the virus, the U.S. was finally thrown into complete pandemonium. It was unbelievable.

Nicholas paid extra attention when she called out the names of the few politicians left. He almost couldn't believe his ears when she mentioned a name that rang at the back of his head, *James Kingston.* How had everyone else either died or turned, yet that spawn of the devil had managed to emerge still safe and sound, probably retreated to his luxurious abode? Why does it always have to be the good guys that get to suffer for others' mistakes? Although, the more Nicholas thought about it, the less surprised he became. That was just what happened when one was powerful enough to have people die in their place, and as a Mafioso in government, Kingston had plenty. He was the type to use anything and anyone to line his pockets and ensure he lived a long, good life.

Nicholas, being one of the tens of thousands of people that had been used by him, didn't know what or how to feel. All that he could feel bubbling up inside of him was utter hatred for the man. If that bastard was alive, then that meant the lab in Guam was still active. Not once in all the years that had passed had Nicholas doubted that it was up and running. As long as Kingston was alive, then the lab would continuously be funded since it provided him a shit ton of money in return.

It angered him that so many people had died in the past twenty-four hours, and that bastard of a man was not one of them. The hatred Nicholas felt was no longer directed at himself but towards Kingston. Nicholas had been obsessed with the idea of revenge for several years. Although he knew it was an inconceivable notion, it was the one drive that kept him going. That even just him being alive was spitting on his face. He could feel his blood boiling as rage surged through his veins, leaving him near tempted to turn off the TV when Jessica shouted.

They all turned their heads to her, and each let out a relieved sigh when they saw that she was still asleep. It was not relieving to know that she had passed out again from the bad news or that she was having a nightmare, but none of them would have known what to do for her if it didn't involve physically defending her.

Nicholas was worried; his animosity towards Kingston seemed to have become a distant memory the instant he moved to the couch and tried to comfort his sister to the best of his power. He couldn't help but feel bad at how incredibly worn out she looked. If before she appeared younger, then at that moment, she seemed several years older, almost as though she had aged twice from grief. No one could blame her. She just had her entire life turned over on its head and battered like a rag. In a matter of minutes, the two people she probably loved most in the world were dead, and she had become an orphan. He wondered what she could have been dreaming of; it couldn't have been too far-fetched. Obviously, it would be the apocalypse and maybe the sight of her mother attacking her father.

Nicholas recalled the death toll that had flashed on the screen of those who had died from zombie attacks all over the country, thinking about how unimaginably high it was. The sight of bodies piled up in the street was just as horrifying as watching the bodies that refused to stay down claw and tear at everyone else. It had only been a day, but the prospect of the horror unfolding around them becoming permanent scared him. Was this going to be their new standard of living? To see each new day, you must fight hordes of zombies.

There were too many people in Jessica's shoes, Nicholas was certain of it. Tragedy didn't discriminate, and if it was not Covid Prime or all its predecessors claiming lives, then it was something else—these new ravenous strains turning people into zombies. It had become a never-ending cycle of suffering, and this time around, there was nothing anybody could do about it. With the President and others dead, and the Vice President's disappearance, then what hope existed for America? For its millions that were suffering? They were done for. Only the top-tier elite that had amassed the means to protect themselves, like Kingston, could afford to sleep at night as though it were just another Tuesday.

There would be survivors, Nicholas believed humans were resilient enough to pull through anything, but he feared that whoever would be left behind would be far too few to rebuild all they had lost. As bitter as it made him, Nicholas was forced to accept the truth. If anyone had a chance at creating a cure, then it would be the monster he had to thank for his immunity, father. All he had done all those years ago was escape. Though he wished he had the strength to raze the godforsaken place when he had the chance, Nicholas knew that if the lab were still in operation at any point in time, then they would have an inkling of how to combat the new virus. Maybe they had not been able to figure it out, but he knew it was only a matter of time. Time he could speed up.

Whatever they had done to Nicholas *had* given him some kind of weird immunity. They had come up with all sorts of crazy psychoactive substances, which they spent years testing on and proving their viability through him and the other kids. He was probably the only one to have survived as long as he did and was dreadfully confident that if they got their hands on the proper research, then they could make a cure. He would not doubt that Kingston must have had something on him to help him escape the White House the way he did. His entire empire revolved around the hard drugs industry, and he would dominate invincibly at the top of it all if he had an underground cure for the disease and its mutant effects. A major win he would not want to lose out on. That pride of his could play to Nicholas's advantage.

The more Nicholas thought about it, the more he believed it was possible. And the more he believed it was possible, the more he felt like he needed to do it. He could get his hands on the cure. He was sure that the location of the lab had not changed. Guam was where illegal activities tied to the U.S. thrived. Kingston had stayed out of the public heat for years, not only because the feds answered his every disposal but because he had a monopoly over a chunk of that extended territory. There was no safer place for the lab to be.

If you can even save the world, then do it.

His father's voice echoed in Nicholas's head again, and he shrieked. He didn't know whether those words pressured him to do something about his worthless life or if it was the heartache he felt at the thought of his half-sister, his colleagues, those who he had killed, or those he had seen get killed. It could be his thirst for revenge, fueled by years of undying hatred towards the politicians that punished him instead of representing and protecting him. It could even be that his thoughts were a weird high that bubbled up from exhaustion. Whatever it was, it gave Nicholas a sense of purpose he didn't think he had ever felt in his life.

Trembling, he wondered if he was still sane for thinking about something as crazy as this. He couldn't stop himself from entertaining the possibility. This was the first time he had ever yearned to do something about his life, the first time he wanted to act for himself.

"What are you plotting?" Diego frowned intuitively. "Whatever it is… I don't like it."

"I don't have a choice," Nicholas replied apologetically; he didn't see the need to beat about the bush.

From the moment he was bitten, Diego had begun to watch him closely. They might have grown distant, but Diego knew him far too well and understood that it was only a matter of time before his sense of duty would have him playing hero.

"You guys," Nicholas said. They looked at him, taken aback by the fierce glint in his eyes. "I know what I have to do."

"And it's stupid," Diego barked, but Josue's eyes lit up with a boyish glee the moment he caught on to the conversation.

"You're going to try and save the world, aren't you." Josue beamed, though his view on the matter seemed a tad too naïve for Nicholas, who nodded in agreement. "Well, then count me in."

"Can you fucking hear yourself," Diego snapped. "This is not some fucking movie. Those are literal zombies out there, and you want to play hero!"

"Diego…" Nicholas called to his surprise, "I'm immune to—"

"I knew you were going to lead with that line. You're full of shit, you know that?" Diego grimaced. "Being immune doesn't automatically make you a savior. No one's asking you to do this."

"But doing so could save millions of lives. If we have a chance at that, then I'm down for anything," Josue insisted to Diego's disdain.

"I'm not asking any of you to tag along with me if you don't want to."

"You're getting a kick out of this, aren't you?" Diego glared at Josue. "It could save millions, but it could also end with us all dead and in vain."

"Watch your tone," Josue growled. It was almost as though, for a split second, something had snapped in him as he took Diego by the corner. Josue had frighteningly become someone else.

Nicholas finally got an answer to the inkling he had always had about his talkative colleague. Josue was never hiding anything; he was just capable of a lot more than his go-lucky demeanor implied. "Enough, you two!" he snapped.

Josue was suddenly apologetic as he gave Diego his space. "It's obvious we're all damn tired... we can talk about it tomorrow when we're all rested."

"There's nothing to talk about...." Diego murmured, storming into the bathroom.

Josue tried to console Nicholas, but he was not exactly receptive to him. Instead, an odd sense of guilt lingered over him as he comforted his sleeping stepsister.

The day went by without event at a torturously slow pace. Josue was restless, and though the television was stuck on the news channel, he remained glued to the couch, eyeing the beautiful reporter on it as though he expected her to turn around and debunk all the tragic news she had already disclosed. Instead, he found himself sinking into a sort of depression as he listened in horror to increasingly unwelcome news.

Eventually, Jessica got up, figuring she needed a shower. Once she was cleaned up and changed, she joined Josue on the couch, depressing themselves with the horrible television. Nicholas couldn't help but notice she had not spoken a word since.

Diego's leg had gotten worse, just as Nicholas feared, and he spent an awful lot of time tending to it so he wouldn't get an infection. When he was done, he hovered over the windows watching the street like an obsessed maniac. He, too, had not said anything else.

Nicholas had been deep in contemplation as he prepared to embark on his adventure, with or without his brother. When he thought time was moving way too slowly, he started to look through their cupboards and refrigerator to see how much they could limit. He was glad to learn that they had enough food to go a couple of weeks, though, by the looks of things, they would have to resort to drinking tap water after the first week. After he had done that, he was embraced by boredom, yet he didn't utter another word as he thought of what he'd say to Jessica, to Diego, to Josue even. Nicholas was still at a loss for words at how quickly Josue jumped at his declaration; it was dauntingly bold of him.

Nicholas allowed himself to simulate whole conversations in his head, and after that, he began to think up goodbyes. After all, he was well aware that the path he intended to take was far too dangerous for him to drag anyone along, especially not Jessica.

Other than Josue's occasional failed attempts at livening everyone else's mood with his usual cheerful demeanor, the apartment was deadly silent. It remained that way till they all had dinner together, and then everyone eventually went to bed for the day, everyone except Nicholas. While they all slept soundlessly, his restless thoughts plagued him, keeping him up till the break of dawn as he anticipated the conversation he was yet to have with Diego and Josue.

CHAPTER SIX

CAPTAIN

Nicholas was careful not to wake Jessica as he crept out of bed early the following day. He had slept on the couch to avoid having a confrontation with his brother before he was ready for it. He put Jessica in his bed so she'd sleep more comfortably, and yet he awoke to her balled up on the couch beside him. It was a tight fit, and it was a miracle he had not knocked her off during the night. In fact, it baffled him that he had not noticed her join him. Nonetheless, he was off the couch and out the front door with the stealth of a ghost.

Once he'd made it outside, he let out a breath he hadn't realized he was holding. Turning around, he locked the door behind him, he was not afraid that Jessica would stir before he got back, but he couldn't risk her stepping out to look for him. He strolled to the end of the hall, right by the stairs that had been barricaded after one of the previous tenants had fallen to their death half a decade ago. Nicholas thought it was scary that he found himself profiting from someone else's tragedy, but none of that mattered at the moment; he had more pressing issues to attend to.

"Took you long enough…." Josue yawned. His hair was an unruly mess, and he still looked drowsy. Obviously, he was not a morning person, and as he stood propped by a counter, he appeared as though he'd

71

tumble over and pass out if they so much as tapped him. Diego, on the other hand, had a sharp stern look in his eyes as he sat on one of the boxes lying about the apartment when Nicholas joined them. They had, at some point, all decided it was best to settle their issue out of earshot while they searched the neighboring apartment for supplies that they could use.

"Thing is, I found some boxes of cereal," Josue started. "I think your sis is gonna love these—"

"That's not what we came here to talk about, is it?" Diego stated. Josue stroked his beard calmly, he didn't say it, but he kind of missed it when Diego used to address him as his superior.

"I've decided I'm going back to Guam." Nicholas broke his silence, startling Diego, while Josue simply stared at the solemn pair with a puzzled curiosity.

"But why Guam? That's so random, *meu amigo*," Josue laughed, shaking his head in bewilderment. He had no idea how grave an issue he was laughing at.

Diego, on the other hand, was slower to respond, peering at Nicholas in wild disbelief. His mouth was agape as though the words he intended had fallen out of him before he could utter them. Simply probing his face, Diego searched for a lining of deceit laced between Nicholas's sharp features, anything to explain his sudden declaration, which Diego likened to an announcement of his insanity.

Nicholas expected a rather more exaggerated reaction from Diego, after all, he was the only one, other than himself, who honestly understood what going back to Guam spelled. Instead, to his surprise, Diego held his hand over his mouth for a moment, pursing his lips, calm in thought like a brewing storm.

While Diego sat in thought, Nicholas bit his lip in a moment of hesitation before he found the courage to say what he had to say, "I think it's possible. What you talked about before…if I could save this fucked up world. I think I can if I go to Guam, and I want to do it. I want to do something for myself. Even if it ends up with me dying, even if it's impossible to get a cure, even if I'm actually more useless than I thought,

I still want to do it. I finally want to do something. I know I can't do it alone, but I don't want to drag you two into this. I don't think there's any harm in trying right now."

"I can't believe it. Nicholas actually listened to me? Nicholas actually took my advice? It's been a good life!" Josue cheered.

Diego cleared his throat loudly, drawing their attention. "You think it's still there, don't you?" he asked sunkenly as Nicholas silently nodded in reply. Josue, on the other hand, was still out of the loop and stared, puzzled at their little understanding. "I understand you have to do this… but I still don't approve of us heading to that godforsaken place—"

"You're not coming with us," Nicholas concluded.

Josue felt as though he had fallen from grace at Nicholas's harsh rejection. "*Buen amigo*, you don't think that's a little tough. He was only against the idea 'cause he was worried about you."

"Don't get me wrong. I can't drag you along with us into hostile territory with a bad leg. Plus, someone has to stay back and keep Jessica safe while we're gone." Nicholas frowned. "You're the only person left alive I can trust with such an important task."

"Sidelining me with praises… that so like you," Diego scoffed. "A hard ass through and through, I guess."

"You make me sound so difficult. I don't think I am in the slightest."

"Well…" Diego laughed.

It was an all too familiar sound that Nicholas had not heard in almost forever. It hit him with a sense of nostalgia about the not-so-good, good old days they had spent together.

As if knowing Nicholas was observing him, Diego sobered up and deadpanned, "But if you two are going to Guam, we need a plan."

They both focused on him, keen on hearing what he had to say next. "With everything happening, I doubt if any flights in the international airports will be operational, especially from all the carnage. The world is in a fucked-up place right now, and nobody wants the other in their country. America is also at the top of the block list. We've been slammed with several travel bans from different countries. Even being in the military doesn't help. We're just mere mechanics; there's not one of us here who knows how to actually man a plane. Even if we did, the McGuire Air Force Base or the Joint Base McGuire Dix Lakehurst is probably out of order. If we would even be allowed to enter, we can't use any of the planes there, and we all know what state those are in. Almost all of the McGuire men were killed yesterday, which means we've lost pilots. Anybody that could literally help us."

"Not everyone, though…" Josue smirked. "If you can get me to a computer, I'm fairly sure I can call in a favor. I still want you both to fill me in on all this Guam shit, though."

"You're going to call in a favor," Nicholas said in shock, ignoring Josue's obvious curiosity. *From whom?*

"Don't sweat it. I have my ways," Josue insisted. "I'm fairly sure I could get us a plane and some firepower while we're at it."

Nicholas and Diego stole a worried glance at each other, but Josue had always been one to come through when the occasion demanded it, so they decided to believe him.

"You could use my phone."

"Like hell, I can," Josue refused Nicholas's offer with an offended look in his eyes, almost as though Nicholas had just made an obvious mistake. "It has to be a secure line, or no one's answering."

"Yeah," Diego concurred, to Nicholas's surprise.

Suddenly, he was the one left out of the loop. "There's a large mall a couple of miles down the street I could drive you two to…but if my guess is right, there's bound to be a gathering."

"I wouldn't have it any other way," Josue smirked with a glint in his eye that spelled trouble; it was more than evident that he was taking all of Nicholas's talk about being heroes far too seriously.

"Hold your horses there. I lost my gun in all the chaos, my crowbar is wedged in a zombie downstairs, and your wrench is out of commission. At the mall, we're going to need a lot more than kitchen utensils and drills."

"Way ahead of you," Josue laughed. It was hard to believe that only a moment ago, he was still drowsy. They watched his glee as he zipped through the apartment, rummaging through boxes. "The hell is it? I swear I saw it," he bickered to himself as Diego and Nicholas simply followed in nervous anticipation.

"Found it!" he cheered out of sight, then strolled back into their view sporting a red ax and a metal baseball bat. "Pretty neat, ey?"

"How the bloody hell did those get there!" Diego exclaimed as Josue handed him the baseball bat and tossed Nicholas the ax. Josue did not reply, smiling smugly as the others were glad that they had gotten their hands on new weapons.

"What about yours?" Nicholas asked as Josue took a black box out from a pile of them, smiling deviously.

"Don't ask… you'll see," Josue sniggered with his usual boyish charm, and yet Diego and Nicholas could not shake the scary sense of foreboding they got from watching him smile.

They had been gone for nearly an hour, and not only had they finally come up with a plausible plan, but they had also found some snacks for Jessica. Nicholas intended for them to sneak back into the room just as they had snuck out, and once they had lined the cupboards, Diego would get the car keys, so they could move out at once. That was until they made it to the room and met Jessica waiting at the door for them like a bored house pet.

"She's up earlier than you said she'd be."

Nicholas wished Josue had bit his tongue as his sister seemed to fume even more after his statement. She frowned sourly at them, tapping her right foot as though she was fighting back the urge to kick him in the shin.

"You left me." Jessica scowled.

"I know… and I'm sorry, but I got you cereal."

"You're not leaving without me." Jessica glared as they all laughed dryly, it was surprising how intimidating a pissed-off teenager could become.

"I am not leaving you." Nicholas smiled reassuringly, but it was far too soon, as the very next moment, she waved the car keys in his face.

Josue nearly leaped out of his skin as Diego buried his face in his palm. Jessica had made it crystal clear that she had listened in on their supposed secret dialogue and had no intention of letting them go, not on their own at least.

"Hell no," Nicholas snapped. "You can't expect me to drag you into this—"

"Fuck that!" she retorted just as fiercely as her half-brother snapped, "You just made me a promise. You can't expect me to stay home. You're taking the short one, and he can barely even work."

Josue was speechless. Diego, on the other hand, was mystified that she referred to him as the short one. Nicholas was worried; it was one thing to take Diego along with him. Diego was a grown man, after all, but Jessica. No. He would not be able to live with himself if anything happened to her.

"It's my father's car anyway…and I hate those things just as much as anyone," Jessica growled with an almost contagious intensity.

Nicholas was still in doubt, their trip was not a joy ride. It was literally life or death.

"I think it'd be better than leaving her home alone. I mean, who knows what could happen?" Diego elbowed Josue's side hard enough it had him groaning.

Nicholas hated that Josue had a point but hated himself even more for contemplating it. He turned to Diego, but the knowing look he got made it clear that the final decision was still his to make. She was his sister.

"Fine," Nicholas admitted through gritted teeth as Jessica lit up with a wicked glint of glee.

"And I'm driving."

"Hell no," Nicholas rebuked, snatching the keys from her, then immediately threw a jacket on, "Get your thickest sweater on, and fast. We're moving out now."

"Huh. It's gonna be like one hundred degrees outside."

"If you're going to head out with us, I want you safe, now do as I say," Nicholas barked, and Jessica bolted over to her bag without another word.

He turned to the others expecting someone to tell him he was wrong, that it was far too dangerous for his sister to be tagging along, yet their reactions were quite the opposite. Josue was obviously excited to head out and kept scribbling what looked like codes into a little notebook he had grabbed off the counter behind them, and Diego was already in the hallway waiting for Jessica to join them.

"Here," Nicholas surrendered, tossing Diego the keys as Jessica darted out ahead, almost as though she was afraid that he was going to lock her in.

Josue took a bit of time, but soon enough, he was out too, hawking his mysterious box along with him. "I'm not telling," he barked at them every time they tried to probe him about the box's contents. Eventually, they simply did not care enough to bother asking. Soon enough, they would all figure it out, somehow.

Nicholas was glad to be home, but the time had come for him to move again, so he decided to take a brief moment to catch his breath, almost as though locking the door had a deeper meaning to it. It felt as though he was sealing their fates with a simple click of a lock.

"Something wrong with the key?" Josue probed as Nicholas realized he was dallying. Without a moment to waste, he locked the door, and soon they were all heading down in the elevator.

Jessica felt sick to her stomach; she was passed out the first time they got on the elevator and so was not prepared to be heading down alongside a lump of rotting flesh. She was obviously disgusted but made a good enough effort to steel herself, unlike Josue, who kept gagging, threatening to blow chunks if they did not get out of the elevator soon. Diego made a little mental note not to use the elevator on their way back up, if they made it back.

Luckily, the hallway was clear, save for what was left of the zombie Josue had left his wrench in. A trail of blood leading out into the driveway explained why there were no zombies present. Once again, Nicholas found himself entertaining guilt for finding the silver lining in the tragedy of another; the difference, however, was that he was not the only one that felt that way for once, but better someone else than them.

They stealthily made their way to the spot where Josue and Nicholas had hidden the SUV. So far, their journey had been a cakewalk. Not to be fooled, Nicholas and Diego clutched their weapons every step of the way. Diego got in the front, like he said he would, and drove them to the mall.

It was all too good to be true. Nicholas hated to be right as the mall came into sight, a horde along with it.

"You ever seen so many?" Jessica quaked in her boots as Nicholas took her hand.

"You don't have to go with us. If you're scared, you can always wait in the car." He hadn't intended to sound condescending, but his statement only seemed to egg Jessica on as she hopped out of the car and shot them an impatient glance.

"We ain't got all day. The sooner we're done, the sooner I can head home."

"Your sis is a real piece of work, buddy," Josue teased to Nicholas's annoyance as they got out of the car.

Jessica noticed that there were fewer zombies at the courtyard leading up to the mall's back entrance, though once they got in, they would all most certainly have to fight their way to the café on the other wing of the third floor. Nicholas worried that Jessica might actually need a weapon, but then Josue smirked.

"She sticks close to me, and we've got nothing to worry about," Josue swore as he finally gave them the grande reveal of the contents of his mystery box. Nicholas was torn between fright and confusion as he watched Josue unveil a plasma power saw, usually used on heavy construction sights.

"Have you lost your fucking mind!" Diego shrieked as the saw buzzed to life, coated in a heated blue hue.

"Chill out. I know how they work," Josue boasted, leading their charge.

They managed to make it to the back entrance without incident, but the door would not budge, well, not until Josue leisurely carved it off its hinges. The usual crisp scent that wafted through the halls had been replaced by the stench of blood, death, and decay, welcoming them as the door blew up dust as it crashed.

"Still think I'm insane?" His annoying voice seemed to haunt Diego as they darted through the large halls of the mall.

The once bright and lively ground floor entertained flashing lights of the various shops and hordes of zombies that had devoured their unfortunate customers. The layout was impressive. Despite the zombies, the mall was still very spacious and well lit. Nicholas was relieved to find that the power was still on.

Their entrance had drawn quite the audience, with a small horde of zombies already stalking them. They avoided the escalators and sharp corners; it would have spelled doom to have a zombie tackle them to the ground when there were already far too many of them in the area. They started searching for an electronics shop that had not been sealed shut yet. Josue could have easily cut through their locks, but Diego feared that that would only alarm the zombies even more.

Though Diego, Nicholas, and Jessica attempted to get through the mall as quietly as they could, Josue had more devious plans. He led their charge, literally carving a path through the zombies as Diego barked directions at them. His eyes lit with an almost frightening animosity as he found a devilish glee in cutting down every zombie in their path. Every shred of sympathy he held towards what used to be human had suddenly become nonexistent in his eyes; he had become the hero's unwavering blade.

They had spent a good amount of time searching for an electronics store where Josue could use a computer, when they were forced to acknowledge that all the computer stores were either sealed up or empty. It was then that Diego had a light bulb moment.

"I know a Café."

"We're looking for computers, not lattes."

"What? No. If I remember correctly, they've got a computer we can use."

"What if they don't," Jessica chipped in as Diego started doubting his suggestion, but Josue was thrilled nonetheless, brandishing his saw as though the cameras about the mall were fixated on his every move.

"We won't find out standing about here. Lead the way, D."

"Don't call me that," Diego scoffed as he darted down a hall with his bat in hand, leading the way.

A small horde had clustered right outside the Café, but sure enough, they could see the computer Diego had mentioned through its showcase. Josue led the charge once again, cutting clean through the rotting flesh of any and all the zombies that got in his path. His swings were long and sloppy, a zombie he had missed hurled itself at him from behind, but Diego was quicker. He knocked it to the ground with a charge before smashing its head in with a single strike to its temple. Josue was startled but grateful. Diego claimed to have done it out of obligation. It was a half-truth. He considered Josue, a friend to his brother and, by default, a friend to himself, so he felt just as obligated to protect him as Josue felt about protecting them all. Honestly, he was glad to be appreciated, even despite the fact that they had fought a few moments ago.

It was a troubling few minutes, but just as their trip to the mall had gone without incident, they made it to the café with a starving horde of zombies circling about the mall in a blind fury.

They can't find us. Jessica sighed in relief as she plopped up against a wall by the window. She and Nicholas had decided to be the lookouts while Josue and Diego got to work on a computer. Jessica frowned at how the once vibrant and energetic stores had been reduced to bloody slaughter rooms. Regardless, everything was going according to plan. All Josue needed to do was work his magic.

Nicholas noticed a play area across from the café they were in and prayed dearly that it was empty before the zombies got there.

Their bold display did not go unnoticed for long. Soon a crowd had begun to build outside the store, so everyone took it upon themselves to barricade the windows and door as Josue kept typing.

"Done," Josue cheered as an invisible weight lifted off all their shoulders.

"Great. Now let's get the fuck out of here."

"Wow… out of here?" Josue called, "We can't leave. He said we should wait for him."

"The hell," Diego chipped. "He's coming here? The whole damn place is crawling with zombies. What good would him coming here do us?"

"He insisted. We've got to hold the fort till he gets here," Josue urged as Diego stared bewilderedly at him. The zombies had already found them and were clawing desperately at the barricade they had made, it was only a matter of time, yet there Josue stood, adamant about convincing them to make a stand against the horde.

"Who's coming?" Jessica probed as Josue itched at the back of his neck awkwardly.

"Jesus Christ. You don't know who it is, do you?" Diego scowled as Josue took his saw and headed for a window. "Answer me, damn it!"

"I don't need to know his name. Don't you get how anonymous chat rooms work? All we got to know is that he's coming," Josue insisted as Diego darted over and grabbed him at the collar.

"Are you trying to get us killed! This isn't a fucking movie. This friend of yours could be screwing with us."

"Diego," Nicholas finally spoke, snapping their attention to him.

Jessica had not uttered a word. Watching them yell at each other scared her just as much as the snarling and growling zombies did.

"If Josue says help is coming, then we've got to believe in him."

"How long till he gets here?"

"30 minutes, tops," Josue swore as Diego finally let him go.

"There's a storage room to the back. Wait in there, and don't come out till I say so, you hear me?" Nicholas said to Jessica. She wiped at her teary eyes and nodded sheepishly, then hurried into the storage room just as her brother had asked of her.

"Guys, our lives are gonna make some really stellar movies," Josue chuckled. The others found themselves laughing with him as Nicholas steeled his mind. Though he felt bad about it, he knew what had to be done.

The first zombie came in through an opening in the window and bounded right at Josue. It was swift, but Josue was faster. All he had to do was hold his saw up as the zombie lunged at him, making mincemeat of its head while spraying him in a thin coat of brain matter.

Three more got in as the front door's barricade gave way. Nicholas swung at the first. The ax he held was alarmingly sharp as it connected with the zombie's neck, decapitating it almost as though the zombie had no bones to begin with. Diego, noticing that Nicholas's first kill with the ax had left him baffled, stepped forward in time to smash one of the other zombie's heads in with a bat, then knocked the other off its feet with another swing before Nicholas brought his ax down on its head, finishing it off. He and Diego shared a moment, they did not say anything to each other, but they had an understanding. Nicholas could swing his ax without a care in the world as Josue did with his saw, confident that Diego was holding up the rear.

Josue was having way more fun than he should have been. He was scared out of his mind and trembling but still had the strength left in him to cackle like a deranged maniac. Diego swung his bat till he was drenched with sweat, and his fingers were covered in bruises, not to mention the dents and blood that every zombie that ran into his range left on his bat. Nicholas saw no end to the madness. The zombies just kept on coming, the barricade still stood, or he was certain they would not have been able to keep up with the waves of zombies darting menacingly at them. So, he did what he could, swinging and hacking at each and every pale-skinned creature that hurled itself at him. That was until he swung again, but his ax did not connect—a zombie had dug its heels into the ground and grabbed his ax mid-swing. Nicholas's eyes widened in horror as the six-foot zombie peered intently into his eyes, a purple foam gathering at the ends of its lip as it growled; it was as though it had stepped right out of a nightmare.

"Fuck. It's one of the hard ones," Nicholas managed to warn before it flung him and his ax across the room as though he weighed no more than a Feather.

"Nicholas!" Diego roared, swinging his bat intently, watching it cave in the side of the zombie's head as his attack connected. Rather than blood, a purple goo seeped out, almost as though its skull was full of jelly rather than a brain.

Diego withdrew in horror as the beastly undead's eye popped out of its socket and fell at their feet, still staring intently at him. It took him by the neck and swept him off his feet in one hand as the weaker zombies swarmed them, eager to devour him as he was suspended in the air. Josue arrived in the nick of time, cutting down three zombies and sawing through the bone and muscle of the zombie's hand as though it was nothing. Diego fell to his feet, coughing and wheezing for air as Josue jumped between them to face the horrid monstrosity, but just as he did, it kicked him in the chest, hard. Josue felt the wind get knocked out of him as he flew straight into a pillar and was knocked out cold. Diego rolled over before the zombie could walk over him and, in the nick of time, got away from a pair of zombies that had pounced at him while he was down. He swung his bat wildly, trying to protect the unconscious Josue and himself. He managed to hit one across the chin, knocking it to the floor, but the other bit down on his bat and wrestled him to the ground.

Nicholas pounced from nowhere, throwing his weight at the zombie to propel his ax deeper into its flesh as he struck it. As fate would have it, his ax cleaved through the zombie's neck and wedged right on its collar bone. To his dismay, the zombie tossed him aside as if he had barely even dented it, then strolled sluggishly towards him with his ax hanging off its neck, which barely managed to stay attached to its body. Nicholas thought he had seen hell, but as the horrid thing strolled towards him, he realized that there was more yet to come. The zombie let out a blood-curdling cry as it barreled towards Nicholas, only for its head to be blown clean off its tattered body right before it could strike.

"Stubborn mou'fuckers ain't ey," a voice jeered from across the room. Nicholas jolted off his back to meet the stranger that had come to his rescue. Where once stood a horde of unrelenting zombies, laid a bloody pile, a red-headed man in an army uniform brandishing his shotgun posed on top of them. They had all been blown apart by shotgun shells, but it startled them that they had not heard a single shot go off until he had killed them all.

"Took your damn time," Josue bickered, wincing in pain as he staggered back onto his feet. He reached for his saw, but the man laughed. "You held 'em off with that. You just as crazy as ya say ya are," the man cheered. He was loud, gutsy, and spoke with an accent that made it tricky for them to tell what he was saying half the time.

"We don't have time for this," Diego groaned as he hurried over to help Nicholas back to his feet.

Josue and the man seemed to be having a moment, like old friends reconnecting after a long winter, but the others were far too afraid of another zombie knocking the wind out of their lungs. "Diego's right. There's going to be more of them heading here after all that noise."

The man heard Nicholas loud and clear, but he smiled blindly as though that little bit of information was irrelevant to him. "You must be the hero." He grinned crookedly. "Call me Captain." Almost simultaneously, the music started, or rather it was at that moment Nicholas noticed it. He could not believe his ears; the music was too damn loud. Nicholas refused to believe anyone in their right mind would be behind it, but Captain and his boys did not count as people in their right minds.

There was music, and a mechanical humming accompanied it. Captain smiled knowingly. "Don't worry 'bout it. I've got ya' all covered." He smirked as Diego returned with Jessica, and together, they all cautiously trailed behind Captain.

Diego was at a loss for words, Nicholas too. Josue had tossed his saw aside without a care in the world, then chatted and laughed over the most trivial and nonsensical things through the halls of the mall. Though there were no zombies in sight, Nicholas could not shake the horrible feeling of dread in the pit of his stomach. It made no sense. The zombies were gone, and instead, a loud mash of orchestra and rock music echoed through the halls the closer to the front entrance they got. Then, the mechanical humming, sounding as though a series of chains were rattling, grew increasingly louder. Jessica clung to Nicholas's arm when he finally stopped dead in his tracks. "What's that noise? Where are we going?" he inquired as Captain smirked and simply went on without them.

"He scares me."

"Me too," Diego concurred with Jessica as Josue scratched nervously at the back of his neck.

"He's like that, but he's actually really funny," Josue explained. "Underneath it all, he's a good guy."

"Good with a shotgun, too," Nicholas remarked as the humming got too annoying to ignore. "The hell is that noise?"

Once confident none of the zombies would jump out at them when they least expected it, they hurried to the front entrance. That's when Nicholas got his answer. The zombies were not gone, they were simply distracted by music coming from the large speakers in the parking lot going off at full blast. The mechanical humming was actually the sound of several Gatling guns attached to a heavily armored military vehicle, going off at once, mowing through the hordes of zombies like they were nothing.

"Took your time." Said Audre as the Captain grinned. "Give me a minute." Just as he said, it took the guns a minute to make mincemeat of what was once a large horde of zombies, shooting the last one down just as the deafening music came to a climax.

None of them were able to describe the feeling that washed over them; it was a splice of fear and intrigue.

"Sorry we're late. It wasn't exactly easy moving this baby through the street," a man chuckled as he hopped over a speaker and hurried over to meet them. "My name's Audre. Over at the car is Diva, and I'm pretty sure you've already met Cap."

"Who are you guys?" Jessica gasped.

Audre was a tall, dark-skinned young man with a bob cut and a boyish charm to his demeanor as he smiled. "We're the guys that are going to help you save the world," he said ever so confidently as Captain patted Nicholas hard on his back.

"Said ya needed ah pair of wings, where we head?"

"Guam," Josue replied sharply. "Don't ask me. Ask them. I've got no idea why we're heading there."

"If you're going there, then I know where you're heading," a blonde lady with a sour frown and a scar at the one end of her lip, Diva, spat.

"You know where we're heading?" Diego gasped as Diva strolled over.

She had a small frame and was barely even taller than Jessica. She was probably not that older either, yet she had an intimidating aura that demanded respect. "Some bastard murdered my parents and snatched me from my home as a kid. If Cap hadn't saved me when he did, I'd probably be in Guam right now."

"A kindred spirit, I guess…." Josue joked as Diva shot him a glare.

Captain had gotten into the car while they were discussing and slammed his fist against the horn. He was the most impatient man on the planet, but if his horn had not gotten their attention, the looming dread of another wave of zombies rushing over did.

"Let's move," Audre said as Josue hurried into their vehicle with them, but Nicholas hesitated. Jessica bit on her lower lip and pretended to be lost in thought, though she wanted so badly to beg him to stay. Nicholas went down on his knee and pulled her into a deep warm embrace. They were estranged siblings a day ago, but they were all each other had, and words could not begin to express how saddening it was that they were parting so soon. "You'll be fine. I'll head right back when it's over."

"Don't fucking die," she sobbed weakly into his shoulder. He was not comfortable hearing her swear, but he guessed that could wait till he got back.

Diego pulled him into a hug soon after Jessica. It shocked him as they hugged awkwardly, but he liked the feeling. He just wished the circumstances were different. "Your brother's going to be waiting for you."

Brother Nicholas could not believe his ears as he watched Diego and Jessica hurry back to the SUV. He hopped onto the back of Captain's vehicle along with the guns, and they escorted the SUV as far as they could to his apartment before parting ways. With his siblings out of the way, Nicholas could focus solely on the task before him, saving the horrible world he lived in.

CHAPTER SEVEN

I WON'T LET YOU

Captain was not a captain. No one knew what he was. What they did know was that he was the right guy to turn to. Three miles south from town lay 20 acres of private property that Captain owned. It was surrounded by an electric fence that ran 24/7, all year long, even before the zombie outbreak. Miles from the walls were nothing but landscape; at the center of it all stood a flashy mansion with a helicopter in its backyard and a giant garage where Captain parked his armored vehicle, right beside a tank he also owned.

"How did no one notice any of this?" Nicholas let out unconsciously as the Captain shot him a glance that spoke volumes yet gave nothing away. It was safe to conclude that the less he knew, the better. They did not waste a beat. Soon as they arrived, Diva and Audre escorted them through the mansion into an armory, while Captain hurried to his helipad to ready the helicopter.

"Wow…" Josue yelled as the lights within the armory came on, revealing an arsenal that ranged from blades to advanced artillery and body armor. On one wall, there were machine guns, rifles, pistols, and two rocket launchers, while the other wall to their right was lined with ammunition, parts, vests, and accessories. Never in all their days had they ever seen so many weapons in one place, and they had both been to the Air force's armory. "*Amigo!* There are enough guns in here to mobilize a small army."

"Hah!" Diva teased. "We're merely borrowing these from Cap's collection."

"Captain loves guns. It's probably why he makes them."

"He makes them?" Nicholas repeated, dumbfounded.

Diva strolled over and handed him a bulletproof vest and pistol. "I'm pretty sure you know how these work, right?"

"Of course we do. Just cause we're mechanics doesn't make us idiots. Now, give me a big one," Josue cheered.

Diva rolled her eyes at him. "Fine. Here," she replied smugly, then took a small piece that fitted perfectly in her palm and tossed it over to Josue. "Big enough for you?"

Nicholas did not realize it at first when he burst into laughter. They all joined in. It felt almost as though none of them were fazed by the implications of the task before them. Audre and Diva were so confident that it made their yet to commence trip to Guam feel like a cakewalk. Suddenly, a bitterness rose up in the back of his throat so strong that it had him arching over a trash can, blowing bloody chunks.

His eyes flew open. Nicholas could not tell how long he was out, but found that he had been moved to a warm bed in a large, sparsely decorated room when he eventually came to. Sitting up to see that his clothes had been changed, he turned to find Josue, who had also gotten a change of clothes, nodding off by his bed. It made him question just how long he was out even more.

Nicholas felt as though his body was burning up and being chewed up all at once. He slipped out of bed in a hurry and staggered into the bathroom so he could see himself in a mirror. He was ghostly pale, and his eyes; there was something wrong with his eyes. His right eye's hue seemed to have faded to a yellowish glow, and his other eye felt numb. He turned his attention to his hand when he noticed the bandage they had neatly wrapped around it. One of them must have tended to his wound while he slept. As Nicholas peeled back the bandage, his eyes widened in horror at the sight of his injury; it was not healing. Rather, purple pus seemed to be gathering at its opening. He did not bother to question what was wrong with him; he had already guessed as much. It felt as though a cruel reality had hit hard, he was not immune to the virus as he thought, he was just slow to the infection.

"They said you needed more rest," Josue worried.

Nicholas scowled at him. "You saw…" he replied. His tone implied it was a question, but he was stating the obvious. Josue's silence spoke volumes. *Hero, my ass, How could I be so naïve?* Nicholas berated himself as he stormed past Josue and back into the room.

"K—"

"I'll rest when I'm dead." Nicholas's reply cut whatever Josue intended to say short as he hurried to get a bulletproof vest over his head. He was not immune, but nonetheless, he could be a key to putting an end to the madness. He could not afford to waste any more time, not when he knew he could become a blood-thirsty corpse at any second.

"Listen to me. You're in no shape for this trip."

"No shit. Obviously, I'm infected," Nicholas snapped, turning to glare daggers at Josue. "I might as well be dead already."

"Don't say that. You're not dead."

"Yeah. Not yet." Nicholas stormed out of the room and darted down the hall with no clear sense of direction; all that mattered to him was that he got away from Josue, who Dashed after him. His head throbbed as a myriad of thoughts berated him. Phil. Jessica. Diego. He could not bear to disappoint them; the idea of it hurt like hell.

"Listen to me," Josue snapped, pulling Nicholas back by his wrist. "The hell do you think you're doing?"

"What I have to," he retorted as Diva and Audre joined them in the hallway.

"You're not thinking straight. We've got to do this together."

"Together." Nicholas was furious. "What's wrong with you? Always trying to insert yourself into my life. Why are you so hell-bent on following me? It's off-putting."

"What's off-putting is you stooping so low. Like I'm just going to walk away cause you're a little mean to me. You're just scared—"

"Of course I'm scared. I'm fucking terrified. I'm infected."

"And you're not a Zombie," Audre chipped in apologetically. "That's a sign if you ask me."

"I'll become one eventually." Nicholas frowned. "I can't waste another moment here."

"Then let's go. My trigger finger ain't happy anyway." Diva yawned.

"NO!" Nicholas protested. "Going to Guam is a suicide mission. I'm already infected, so it's good if I die alone—"

"We have a saying in this house," Captain's voice Bellowed from the room Diva and Audre came from as he strolled out to meet them, "Live and let me die."

"If you're going to die, it's fine. If you want to live, even better. But you're not going to decide where we die," Diva added.

Something caught Nicholas's attention. There was a low growling coming from the room behind Captain, who must have noticed Nicholas's wandering eyes and obliged him with a peep, stepping aside and gesturing at him to go in. Audre and Diva moved away willingly, letting Nicholas feed his curiosity as he investigated incautiously, with Josue following shortly behind him. The room had several hospital drapes about it and smelled strongly of disinfectants. The closer he got, the colder it got, and the sooner he heard the beeping. He found a UV and heart monitor plugged beside a bed at the end of the room. In the bed lay a little girl, barely over the age of six, strapped to its frame with an oxygen mask over her face. Nicholas felt his heart sink as he noticed the bite mark on her wrist.

"She's Captain's granddaughter," Audre explained. "She couldn't make it to the fence on time. Right before the captain could get to her, a zombie bit her." In comparison to all the other zombies he had encountered, she had barely begun to turn. "Thankfully, sedating her managed to slow her change… but we can only keep her sedated for so long before it becomes fatal."

"She's infected…does that make her dead too?" Diva scowled as Audre shot her a stern look. "You might think Cap is some savior, but he's human too. You're here 'cause he thinks you're his last chance at salvation—"

"That's enough, D," Audre barked as he caught her mid-sentence, and Diva left the room.

Nicholas fought the overwhelming guilt that drove him to tears then and there. He felt so torn between his depression and the pressure mounting every second that went by. It Caused him to kneel in exhausting.

Josue stood behind him; he was not offended, he could not even begin to comprehend what Nicholas was going through, and so instead, he decided to quietly wait for him to calm down.

"Josue…" Nicholas called softly, "I'm sorry."

"I know you are." Josue grinned, helping Nicholas to his feet.

Nicholas felt like he was getting weaker with every passing breath. It was difficult for him to admit it, but he knew for a fact that the task at hand was far too great for him to see through on his own.

The moment they stepped out of the room, they met Audre, Captain, and Diva, fully dressed in black body armor and armed to the teeth with guns and knives.

"I know what's in Guam." Captain smirked, "We're going da get ya cure. Then burn dat lab to da ground."

"And we don't need your permission," Diva scoffed.

Where we live or die is ours to decide.

Nicholas did not know why he heard that in his father's voice, but he understood the message. "I'm ready when you are," he assured the others as they all made their way to the helicopter, primed to commence their mission at once.

Pain. The pain was mind-numbing. So much so that it would make any regular person beg for death. Nicholas could not tell if it was motion sickness or if his insides were actually churning all through the flight.

"You good, buddy? You don't look so good," Josue worried.

Nicholas smiled. "I'm fine. Just a little motion sickness," he lied; he could feel the virus eating at him from the inside. It hurt like hell, but if time were to turn back to that moment before the elevator, he was confident that he would still throw himself in the way to save Diego and Jessica.

"Josue…" Nicholas said. "If I ever turn. Kill me."

Josue understood him loud and clear but did not want to entertain the thought, so he pretended not to have heard him. They all sat in an awkward silence that seemed to stretch on to eternity before the Island, Guam, finally came into view.

"You're sure they have a cure?" Diva probed.

Nicholas groaned from getting his parachute on. "I know they will. Problem is getting it off the island."

Nicholas frowned as they all smirked back at him. "That's where we come in," Audre replied.

The coast was crawling with zombies, and Captain was not confident about landing, so they had to find a clear enough spot to parachute from. It took them a while; the helicopter's propellers kept attracting hordes of zombies, so finding a place was rather difficult. Right before their jump, Captain handed Diva a small device that Nicholas couldn't make out, but he didn't think too much about it. It was straining enough to stay conscious as they hurled themselves out of the helicopter.

Josue and Diva made it to the ground first, gunning down the few zombies that had circled about their landing area before Nicholas and Audre joined them. They took a moment to check on their gear when suddenly, Diva vanished into the woods carrying most of their weapons.

"Where's she going?" Josue demanded

"Cap's got other plans for her. I'll get you both to the lab. Nicholas."

"Oh…right," Nicholas stirred. His vision felt foggy, and so did his thoughts.

Josue and Audre were worried. For his sake, they prayed their encounters would be fewer. Their hopes were dashed when their mission turned into a race a few seconds later.

Nicholas could barely hold his aim and fell over after the recoil from his pistol dazed him. He was like a toddler learning how to walk. If Josue and Audre were not with him, the mission would have been a failure before it had even begun.

"Focus on running; we'll cover you," Audre and Josue concurred.

Nicholas complied. As he ran, he struggled to retain consciousness; it became difficult to tell if he was even on the right track, but he knew the path leading to the lab. In his delirious state, it felt as though he was fleeing the lab instead of running right back to his captors. Nothing had changed. The river that washed him to shore was still there; the only difference was that it had a dead zombie floating in it. Following the river uphill, he met the steep climb he had tumbled down all those years ago. For a moment, it felt as though the scars from that very fall had reopened.

"Keep moving," either Audre or Josue yelled over the snarls and growls of the zombies pursuing them.

Nicholas dug his fingers into the dirt, pulling himself up the hill while his companions fired wildly into the growing crowd of zombies behind him. He made it to the top, and with a bloody nose and an unrelenting thirst, he sprinted through the woods. For a split-second, Nicholas could have sworn that rather than zombies, he was being chased by the dogs that nearly mauled him the night he escaped. He could almost smell their musk as they gained on him.

Coming through the clearing, Nicholas lost all sense of himself. He could not hear Josue or Audre, not even his panting. He could not feel his feet or the cut on his cheek, which he got from brushing against a rough tree. Eventually, his sight became a blur as he ran into the electric fence. The lab must've installed it to keep any more children from escaping after he did.

CHAPTER EIGHT

I WILL NEVER LEAVE AN AIRMAN BEHIND

Everything felt empty, pointless. Alive or dead, Nicholas could not tell what he was. For all he knew, he could have been undead. It was blissful at first, but only for a very brief moment, then doubt began to fill his mind. He was not asleep, but he was not awake either.

"*Nicholas*," a voice called desperately. Who is that? Even when it stopped, he could still hear it.

"*Nicholas*." It sounded familiar. It felt as though he was supposed to know what it meant, who it was.

"*Wake up, Nicholas!*" another voice insisted in the distance.

His doubt was suddenly replaced with rage, a pointless anger that he did not appreciate. Nicholas was his name, he could remember that much, but he could not remember who told him the words '*If you can even save the world, then do it.*'

Why was everybody yelling at him? Why did he feel so sleepy? What was happening? A million questions, a million voices. Soon his head felt like it was locked in a heated debate with himself.

"I'm glad you've come. We finally have use for you, *Neno*."

"Father!"

Nicholas woke with a spring fueled by blind rage as a voice he dreaded addressed him. His eyes blazed a yellow hue that did nothing to hide his anger. The fatigue and pain he had felt were gone. In their place was a deranged rage. He glared across the lab, from the table he was strapped down to, at Dr. Actassi, who was tinkering with the vials before him.

"Oh, goodie… I'm glad you're awake." Dr. Actassi smiled fondly at him.

"Fuck you," Nicholas growled, tugging at his restraints. He could not explain how fury had overcome his reason, but he had the overwhelming rage to kill the doctor, to eat him.

"I see…" Dr. Actassi noted. "You're very much sane but driven by the virus' impulsive urge to devour flesh, either that or you're just glad to see me."

The man before him was crooked, old, with an almost entirely grey head of hair, but even on the fine line between sane and insanity, Nicholas could tell he was the father that put him through hell all those years ago.

"To hell with you!"

Nicholas thrashed and barked like a deranged maniac as the doctor eyed him intently. He probed Nicholas from a safe distance before putting something in a syringe and then approached him. "Who would have thought that out of hundreds, you would be my greatest breakthrough?" Dr. Actassi cackled. "I've created a drug to delay the effects of the virus, but your body did that all on its own."

As the doctor spoke, he drew in too close to Nicholas, just as he wanted him to. Nicholas seized the opportunity, snapping off one of his restraints like it was made from thin rubber, and grabbed the doctor by his throat. Nicholas's eyes lit with a bloodthirsty glee. He began to salivate at the thought of how it would feel to let the rage lead him to bite down on the evil doctor's jugular. Nicholas struggled to control himself as he tightened his grip, watching the doctor's face turn blue. Then, when he least expected it, Dr. Actassi stuck a needle into his neck, emptying the syringe's content directly into his bloodstream.

Dr. Actassi fell to the floor, choking and gasping for air, but moments later, he was laughing maniacally. Nicholas felt as though a jolt of lightning surged through his body as he convulsed in pain, but soon he felt calmer, weak, as though he had been given some anti-depressant. "What did you do to me?"

"Here I thought I'd have to concoct a cure from scratch, the process could have taken me years, but instead, fate delivered the quickest fix to my doorstep. Alas! Rejoice, my boy! You're the first person to be cured," Dr. Actassi laughed. "But no one will know."

"You, monster," Nicholas growled.

The doctor took out his phone to make a greatly confident phone call. "You're in luck, Mr. President. I've got your cure," he boasted. "I'll have it at your bunker by noon. I expect my requests have already been met."

"Huh," Nicholas groaned. "The President's dead."

"Oh yes, your President is. I was on the phone with his replacement." Dr. Actassi smirked, inserting a needle in Nicholas's neck to draw blood.

Nicholas believed what the doctor had said, he was feeling much better, but he was worried about his companions, Audre and Josue, and troubled by the phone call he had just eavesdropped on. "You won't get away with this... I won't let you."

"Boy, you're too naïve. I have no use for you now," he taunted, leaving Nicholas alone in the room.

Dr. Actassi was so shaken by Nicholas's attack and blinded by his pride that he had forgotten that one of Nicholas's restraints were undone. Once he was alone, Nicholas quickly freed himself from the restraints holding his other arm and legs. His clothes were scorched; just then, he remembered he had run right into an electric fence before passing out. In fact, it was a miracle he was unscathed.

Nicholas got out of the bed just as a guard came in to check on him. The man, shocked to see him free, could not react in time to stop Nicholas from wrestling him to the floor. The guard was twice his size and put up a hell of a fight, but Nicholas had no trouble pinning him to the ground with one hand long enough to disarm him and knock him out with his free hand the very next second.

"Wow..."

Nicholas was undoubtedly more robust than he remembered, an apparent lingering side effect from the virus. His fingers still felt numb from whatever the doctor had injected him with, yet he could summon more strength into them than ever before. Nicholas could not tell for sure how long the effects would last, but one thing was certain, he needed to find Audre and Josue, then get the hell out of Guam. He was confident that they were being held in one of the many rooms within the facility, and he had a wild guess where. It had been ages, but most of the halls' layouts were still ingrained in his memory. He had no time to lose; he had to find the others, get the cure, and escape from the facility once again.

After concocting a plan in his head, he was preparing to leave when a tremor ran through the building, causing a blaring alarm. *An Explosion*! He panicked as soon after the echo of yells and gunfire stirred him, crowds of staff hurried out into the hallways. Nicholas, seeing no better opportunity, stepped out and joined the shuffling feet as they raced to the exit, but just then, they all halted and desperately tried to head the other way. Nicholas was puzzled as they pushed and shoved until he fell to the ground and saw the terror for himself. Before the scared crowd was zombies, zombies of the children they had tortured and experimented on. As Nicholas darted in the opposite direction, he stumbled across a room with familiar faces strapped down inside it.

"Nicholas! You're alive." Josue beamed ecstatically as Nicholas made quick work of his restraints, then hurried over to help Audre out of his. "And you look great!"

"I got the cure—"

"There's a cure?" Audre jumped at him, "Where is it? Please tell me you got it."

"I couldn't. The bastard who made it ran off with it."

"Fuck! What do we do now?"

"We've got to find him before he gets out of the facility."

"I've got an idea of where he might be heading," Nicholas replied.

"Then lead the way." Audre smiled just as the door was blown off its hinges by the weight of a guard that had been shot into it. Audre swiftly armed himself with a knife from his boot, though he doubted it would help him in a gunfight.

They were all relieved to watch a pissed-off Diva stroll into the room. "Sorry I'm late," she sighed, tossing them a bag filled with guns. "The security wouldn't listen to reason."

After Audre rushed over to hug Diva, they all armed themselves and were back in the hallway when a zombie girl crept towards them. Diva was quick on her feet and would have shot the girl had Nicholas not thrown himself between them. All of them were surprised and on edge but watched as not one but two zombie children approached Nicholas, sniffed, then darted past like they were invisible.

"You've got superpowers now!" Josue shrieked as they darted through the bloody halls of the lab.

Nicholas was not in the mood to explain what happened, though he laughed at the thought of the cure leaving him with superpowers. He'd noticed the zombie children within the facility were more competent than the others they had encountered, intently going after only doctors and guards. So long as they did not trouble the zombies, they could move through the halls as though they were all shadows.

They made it to the private office at the end of the facility. To Nicholas's dismay, the door was open. He feared that they had arrived far too late, but as he walked through, he learned how horribly wrong he was. On the table was the cure they had come for in a tiny serum bottle. At the center of the room lay its maker, slowly being devoured by five children.

"Jesus Christ," Josue gasped in horror as the doctor held out his fingerless hand to plead for help. He could not call to them; one of the children had pulled out his tongue just as another had chewed off his fingers and thrust a pencil in his right eye. Nicholas glared at the doctor as the children stared intently at them until he shut the door behind him. He hoped that in seeing the last moments of the monster that had traumatized him, he would finally be able to move on.

"They weren't zombies, were they?" Josue grimaced, but the others were content with getting the cure and darted out as fast as possible.

Once out of the facility, they were back to fighting their way through hordes of zombies. Rather than using the coast they came in through, they tried to make it into town. Diva found a car with a key in it by chance, and with it, they made their daring escape. They managed to get a reasonable distance between them and the zombies when the car ran out of gas, not too far from a bridge.

"Radio to breaker, this is Diva; Radio to breaker, this is Diva. Over," Diva called into the radio Captain had handed her before their descent.

There was static as Captain's frantic voice came through, "The hell are you guys?"

"On foot on route to our rendezvous point."

"Screw the rendezvous, get to cover. I've got bombardier jets heading at your location."

Diva froze dead in her tracks as she finally noticed the jet homing in on their location. "Everyone. Get cover!" she cried out, but there was no cover in sight.

CHAPTER NINE

EVEN HEROES HAVE THE RIGHT TO BLEED

The first bomb took them all by surprise; it had exploded some meters away from where they stood, and they were swept up in the wind by its shockwave, forcefully tossed about like ragdolls by the sheer might of the blast. Luckily, the bombs that followed missed them entirely.

Nicholas took the worst of the explosion; he was right in front of the group when it went off. Nicholas watched his life flash before his eyes as he was hurled through the air. Slamming hard against a car, hitting his head so hard it left him concussed, he fell to the floor with a loud thud. The serum bottle he clutched, their last hope was very nearly lost as it had flown out of his hands-on impact, but he quickly caught it before it could roll away from him, or worse, shatter. Bruised, bloodied, and tormented by the traumatic ringing in his ears, he dragged himself back onto his feet groggily. The heat had scorched him, though by some string of luck, the burns had not been too dire. Even if they were, he had no time to lick his wounds. It was a slow and grueling process, but there was no time to waste, too much was at stake, and the fate of many demanded that he survive. There might not have been that many left to save, tragically, but the people outside waiting on him were more than enough.

Nicholas hesitated; it was a miracle he had survived the first blast, a miracle that did not seem too likely to repeat itself if he were to hurry on blindly. He stoped to take a moment to regain his bearing and assess the mess he had found himself in. As it seemed there might not be a repetition of the blast, he swiftly stole the opportunity to rush over to his teammates. Nicholas, through it all, had still refused to allow himself to become accustomed to death as he checked on them, making sure they were okay, unwilling to let another person die on him. Audre and Diva seemed to be fine, but Josue was not moving. Nicholas needed everyone safe and sound, so it was a relief to watch Josue cough and wince in pain as he shook him.

It took him a moment, but eventually, Nicholas realized his right eye had been nipped, blurring his sight with blood, but he forced it open. The almost mind-numbing pain was accompanied by an unbearable throbbing at the back of his head, but he endured it, still searching eagerly through his teary left eye for a glimmer of hope. Flames had engulfed the path before them, and behind them came the agitated groans of the horde drawing far too close for comfort. Nicholas's search was not in vain, he thought he had noticed another passage they could take to the far left of the street down a tunnel.

Nicholas frantically hurried Josue and the others along with him, only to be halted at a pit of despair. They were running out of safe options to get away from their impending doom, and their only other choice was the tunnel he had noticed, but they just discovered it had been blown shut. They couldn't see the other side of the barrier, but then again, they could not afford the luxury of time if they intended to dig their way through it. The jet would soon circle back and blow them all to bits along with the zombies. The blast that had disoriented Nicholas and the others had caused the entrance to cave in on itself. It would take forever to get through the debris, and there was not enough time, Audre concluded.

Nicholas was lost in thought, his head hurt like hell, but that did not stop his brain from working hard at coming up with their next course of action. With everyone depending on him, he decided to calmly pace as he pondered a solution. The route they had intended had been blown to bits before their very eyes, and the only other passage left was impassible. There was no other choice left to make, but they were not willing to give in to despair yet. They had one more option. They had to turn back.

"We've got to head back to the lab."

"That blast must have done quite the number on you, Hero," Diva spat.

"The facility had a helipad with no helicopter," Nicholas insisted. "If we radio Captain in now, I'm fairly sure he'd make it to the lab before we do, then he can easily get us from the roof—"

"You don't get it. I rigged the whole bloody place to blow. Captain's orders," Diva retorted, but Audre and Josue saw reason in his suggestion and did not hesitate to take Nicholas's side.

"We're sitting ducks out here if that jet realizes we survived and circles back. How long do we have?" Audre demanded.

Diva panicked, rummaging through her suit before she decided to make a wild guess. "30-35 minutes tops!" She snapped. "We'll never make it in time."

"Not with that attitude," Audre replied cockily from the front seat of a torn-up Audi he had managed to hot-wire while she was distracted. The car was big enough to fit them all, but it had not survived the blast entirely, one of its doors was blown off and it was missing half its roof, but all that was compensated by the fact that it had a full tank of gas.

"What about the zombies?" Josue croaked as Nicholas helped him into the vehicle, he had not sustained anything other than a few burns here and there, but they could tell the blast had done just as much a number on him as it did the rest of them.

"We can worry about that later. Now, just drive," Nicholas replied as everyone got in the car, and Audre zipped back down the street they had just come from.

Just as Nicholas had suspected, the jets had not intended to fire on them; they were dealing with the zombies' alarming numbers; the legion of burnt zombie carcasses littering the street was a testament to his claim.

Even then, their zombie problem was far from over. Yet another mob came into sight a matter of minutes from the others the jet had decimated.

Josue could barely stand up, but he got an idea. "How much firepower do we got?" he yelled.

"Why'd you ask?" Diva furrowed her brows at him as he reached forward and helped himself to an assault rifle from a bag that she clutched.

"We're going to smoke our way through," he replied cockily, a smug grin on his face.

Nicholas was dumbfounded, but he could not resist his urge to laugh as he and Diva joined Josue. Nicholas would never admit it, but he thought to himself that at that moment, Josue could pass as an action movie star with his almost frightening ideas.

Diva had her doubts, but rather than voice them, she joined in as Audre drove like a literal mad man, trying to ram into as few obstacles as he had to. Josue, Diva, and Nicholas tried to shoot as many zombies as they could. What seemed like a farfetched idea at first had become their saving grace. Their guns mowed through crowds of zombies, causing the others behind them to trip over and fall to the ground. Before any of the zombies could get back up, the Audi had simply run them over as though they were a makeshift ramp, and any that got too close to the driver seat had its brains blown off quicker than they could so much as startle Audre. It was a grueling and literally bumpy ride through the city.

They had run out of ammo and resorted to throwing grenades that nearly toppled the very vehicle they were fighting desperately to protect when Audre ran through the last zombie in their path and made it onto a clear route.

"20 minutes and counting," Diva reminded them with a cheer in her voice as they all began to howl and laugh like wild animals. They were far from out of danger, but Audre and Josue felt celebrating their little victories was just the motivation they needed.

Diva's radio crackled to life as just the man they needed to talk to called, "Diva! Diva! Where you heading!"

"Change of plans, Cap. Head to the Lab. I repeat, we're on route to the bloody lab!"

"But da bombs—"

"We'll make it, Captain. You've got to believe us!" Nicholas interrupted from the backseat as Captain's maniacal cackle filtered through the radio.

"Hero, yeah! I got you!"

A few minutes later, they spotted his helicopter en route to the lab ahead of them. Just as Nicholas had said, Captain would be hovering over the building in time to pick them all up.

"Now, all we've got to do is make it there," Josue gulped, stealing the words straight out of Nicholas's head as he glared at the timer. They had 12 minutes left to make it through the lab, and it was yet to come within their sights.

"Oh no," Audre gasped.

"What does 'oh no' mean?"

"The brakes are deader than the last person that drove this heap of shit," Audre deadpanned just as the lab came into view. "We're gonna have to brace for impact," he warned.

Nicholas managed to get Josue's seatbelt on as Audre swerved right towards the entrance, but when he returned to his, he realized his seat belt would not buckle. They were moments away from impact, and Nicholas was certain he would not survive it. Without a seat belt, the vehicle would hurl him hard against the wall, and his neck would certainly snap. He had been tossed about far too many times already, so instead, he threw himself out of the car before it crashed.

Nicholas struggled to get back on his feet. He was dizzy, but he was alive. It was While he was recovering, he learned that Diva had done the same thing, but unlike him, she did not stop to lick her wounds. Rather, she glanced at her timer and yelled at the top of her lungs. "Nine fucking minutes left! Move it!"

Josue and Audre got out of the vehicle. Audre had a bloody nose from the car's airbag, but he was glad it cushioned the impact, considering how worse it could've been. Josue, on the other hand, had severe whiplash, but he darted down the halls too. Diva led their race. With nine minutes to spare, she could hear the helicopter loud and clear, just as clearly as she could hear the bomb's timer ticking diligently about the lab.

Nicholas was at the rear darting up the stairs when he caught something out of the corner of his eye and went into a trance. He had not realized how severely concussed he was when he let the illusion of his younger self lead him astray.

Meanwhile, the others had gotten on the chopper by the 2-minute mark. It was not until they had buckled up that they realized Nicholas was not accounted for aboard their escape vessel.

"The hell is he?" Captain yelled.

"He was right behind you."

"The hell do you mean he was right behind me? We got here at the exact same pace!" Josue returned to Audre in a blind panic. His mind was boggled as he undid his buckle. He was willing to rush back into the lab had Audre and Diva not caught him.

"Take your bloody time, Hero!" Diva jeered just as Nicholas emerged upon the roof, clutching a giant case file to his chest as he darted clumsily towards the jet.

Diva had been a bit off with her estimate, but luckily, they had made it to the chopper on time, but that did not change the fact that, with the cure they had risked their lives to retrieve, Nicholas was running toward them with barely 30 seconds left on the clock. Nicholas, concussed, hurled the file through the air, watching as it barely made it onto the chopper, then jumped in time to grab Josue's hand as it took off.

Desperately making it out of the lab's blast radius, narrowly escaping getting blown out of the sky, they watched the lab be reduced to nothing. They had finally made it out of Guam. The blast from the lab's destruction was deafening, but not nearly as deafening as the cheers from everyone in the chopper as they made off with not just the cure to the virus, but proof of the horrible experiments Dr. Actassi and his men had carried out. It felt like a dream.

"You're a madman, K!" Audre cheered as he and Diva locked lips passionately. Josue looked on a tad jealous, but he had suspected they were either lovers or siblings from how close they were.

Nicholas did not want to bring it up, but his ears rung, and his arm hurt like hell, not to mention the blood on his bandage was a clear sign his wound had reopened. "You look like shit," Nicholas joked when he noticed how intently Josue eyed him. It was more than obvious he was still very worried about his well-being.

"You must feel like shit," Josue commented.

"Of course I do," Nicholas laughed as he powered through his pain to stretch an arm out and shake Josue's hand. "What sort of Wingman would I be if I didn't feel as horrible as you looked."

Wingman! It had a nice ring to it. Josue's eyes lit up with glee, and rather than a handshake, he pulled Nicholas into a bear hug. Captain was enjoying a smoke, but he let them take a bottle of whiskey from right under his seat. They were one step closer to saving the world. Nicholas could not wait to get back to Diego and Jessica. He had so much to tell them, and though his body felt as though he had just been pulled through a wringer, for the first time in years, he was genuinely happy. Not only had he faced his demons, but he had also made his father proud.

Next stop. HOME.

EPILOGUE

DADDY IT'S OVER

It had been two weeks since her brother and his colleague had gone to 'Save the world'. Jessica and Diego had come up with a new sort of system. The crazy old man from the mall had given Diego an idea. He drove the SUV down the street and hooked it up to a giant speaker to play jazz music for most of the day, so they felt safe knowing there were no zombies within the building.

Jessica noticed that Diego had become somewhat overbearing. He always wanted her to be within his sight during the first few days of Nicholas's absence. She hated it, hated the restriction it placed on her, making her feel like she was a child that needed constant protection or a damsel in distress constantly in need of saving. Eventually, she began to understand him, seeing it from his point of view. Diego tried not to give it away, tried his best to affect an air of courage and control, but he was still worried, and he was worried that she would discover his worry. He did not realize that she had not only noticed his fear, but she felt the same way

Diego was trying his best to look out for her in the way he felt her brother would. He rarely let her out of the apartment. If he had his way, she would never have to kill a zombie, though it was far too late for that. The very night they returned from the mall, after her brother's departure, she was overcome with wanderlust to quell her loneliness and curiosity. She had snuck out of their apartment, where she was ambushed, forced to kill a zombie on the staircase a floor below their apartment. Luckily for her, there was only one, or she could have easily been overwhelmed and eaten alive. Diego would not have been able to live with himself.

Eventually, Diego started to talk more, and they both began to get along. He had a lot of stories about her brother, good, bad, and ugly. It gave them both hope to sit at the dining table and pretend everything was well. His stories gave her hope that Nicholas would walk through the apartment door when they least expected it. Since he had accidentally left with the key, they were practically living without a lock on their door, so she was going to scold him about that as soon as he returned.

When Diego ran out of stories, he found a board game that they could play, and when she was too bored for board games, they would stuff their faces with junk food and beer, one of the many perks they enjoyed from raiding the mall that day. Diego was cool. Jessica did not have to waste any effort to convince him to let her drink, though it was only on the mutual agreement that she was not allowed more than two bottles a day and that their little secret remained between them.

In the following days, when Diego was alone, he would be glued to the couch, hoping for any news of a cure or a sign that they were all alive and well. His routine was depressing, though Jessica could not blame him. After all, unbeknownst to him, she did the same thing too. She would jump at the television first thing in the day and then again right before bed. Sadly, news of their brother's achievements never made it to the big screen.

At some point, Jessica doubted he was ever coming back and would cry herself to sleep, then she would hate herself for thinking that way. Almost simultaneously, she and Diego both started to lose track of time. They slowly grew into a repetitive schedule where all they did was eat, pray, sleep, and talk on the few occasions they felt like it. Their lives had become exceedingly mechanical. To help with her boredom when everything felt bleak, she and Diego would explore the other apartments.

Though every room they explored only left her feeling more depressed than before they set out to begin with. It became a habit of theirs.

By the second week, Jessica had taken on a cheerier demeanor. Having fewer zombies prowling about the apartment building had given her a false sense of security. Diego's leg had healed, and he spent most of his newfound free time working out on the roof, both as a way of keeping his body and mind fit. He had to be prepared for the possibility of an intrusion or crisis, most especially because they barely had a door.

Diego was not in the room when the usual news broadcast came on, the same time it did every other day, but this time, something was different. The beautiful reporter was smiling. Not her usual forced expression as though out of a sense of duty, but this time, her smile radiated in such a way that filled Jessica with a nostalgic glimmer of hope. Seeing that lit a torch under her feet as she hurriedly hopped off the couch and stuck her head out the window so she could call out to Diego at the top of her lungs. She could not tell for sure if he had heard her, but she did not want to leave the apartment for even a second. She did not want to miss what she expected to be great news.

"If he hasn't heard me, that's his loss," she said to herself haughtily as she hopped back onto the couch and hugged the pillow tightly against her chest. The reporter started, as usual, delivering her daily dose of despair with insights into the ever-growing anarchy across the state as well as how high the death toll had risen.

Jessica thought the death rate would eventually hit a peak and then drop afterward. On the other hand, Diego believed that after the mortality rate had peaked, it would remain there for a while before dropping. Then assuming newer states of equilibrium, the cycle would continue on and on until the rate of mortality dropped, eventually to zero, or at least to a figure infinitely close to that. The thought of it all still horrified Jessica.

She observed the reporter speak of a conspiracy revolving around a famous politician of sorts.

"He's dead," Diego gasped at the door as a wicked grin grew across his face. "That Kingston bastard Nicholas won't shut up about is finally dead."

The reporter narrated the news on Kingston's prolonged infection before his fall to the undead. Then the Vice President was invited, via video coverage, to share his accounts of the horrors that unfolded within the White House and about how Kingston and his guards had kidnapped him and confined him to a secret cell on one of his estates for the past week. He also commended the valiant efforts of a small makeshift band of mercenaries who had unraveled the conspiracy and rescued him. Jessica did not care about the Vice President, Kingston, or any of their stories. She refused to believe that the glint in the reporter's eyes was simply because a few evil men had gotten what they deserved.

Diego was gushing with glee, but Jessica was never a fan of the news. She was far too young to see the big pictures that every line uttered by the reporter painted to the people. When the suspense began to eat at Jessica, the camera panned back to the reporter, who had been moved to tears. Tears of joy. She was not crying because the Vice President had made a safe return, Jessica could tell. The reporter had held up a potent guise for so long and was finally relieved enough to let her genuine emotions surface as she cleared her throat and spoke. It felt as if time stood still. The reporter talked about how the UN had received breaking news of a cure.

"We did that, you know," Josue's voice broke the silence as he and Nicholas snuck into the apartment and crept up on them. Jessica spun to face them so quickly she gave herself whiplash while Diego dropped the beer he had gotten to celebrate the news of Kingston's fall to the infection. Diego rushed over to hug his brother just like he had done when he saw him off while Jessica stood dead in her tracks as if she had seen a ghost.

"Jessica?" Nicholas called as she threw herself over the couch, tumbling to the floor roughly. Surprised, he hurried to her, but despite her bruise, she lunged at him again, running her hand through his unruly nappy head of hair as she hugged him tightly. It felt climatic, like a weight she never realized was there had been lifted off her chest.

"You came back... you came," Jessica chanted deliriously as Nicholas hugged her. It felt like a dream. She refused to let go of him despite how awfully uncomfortable the position she was hugging him made them both. It was as though if she let go, even for a nanosecond, he would disappear, and she would wake up alone on the couch like every other time she had dreamt of his return.

"I'm here… I made it," Nicholas cooed softly as he patted her head, and she finally let all the emotions she had bottled up swell and erupt through tears.

"It's over. Daddy, it's over. We made it," Jessica whimpered as she cried in her brother's arms.

Nicholas thought he was not going to cry, but Jessica had managed to get him emotional enough to cry like a child. It was finally over; he was home. Though he was sure it would take much longer before the cure could get around the world. Nicholas could finally smile, knowing he had Josue to always liven the mood. Diego, to keep him in check, and his beloved stepsister, Jessica, to look after. It did not matter what life had in store for them. Together they were ready to face anything.

ABOUT THE AUTHOR

Staff Sergeant Patrick Sims (retired) was born into a family of 7 children and raised in Milwaukee, Wisconsin. He served for 13 years in the United States Air Force, being deployed to both Iraq and Afghanistan during his military career. He is the founder of Wounded Healers, LLC (wounded-healers.org) and Invisible Wounds, a nonprofit organization focused on healing the invisible wounds of war and active duty.

Additionally, SSgt Sims supports active-duty members and veterans who combat anxiety. He is also invested in suicide prevention and other vital mental health services for current and former service members.

SSgt Sims resides in Virginia with his wife. He is the father of two boys.

www.ingramcontent.com/pod-product-compliance
Lightning Source LLC
Chambersburg PA
CBHW051232210726
48290CB00003B/926